The Growing Season

The Growing Season

A NOVEL

JANE LORENZINI

Published by Nest Press, Nashville

Edited and designed by Girl Friday Productions
www.girlfridayproductions.com

Design: Paul Barrett
Project management: Kristin Duran
Editorial production: Katherine Richards
Image credits: Shutterstock/Andrii Salomatin (front),
University of Tennessee Libraries (back)

ISBN (hardcover): 978-1-7323248-5-5
ISBN (paperback): 978-1-7323248-3-1
ISBN (ebook): 978-1-7323248-4-8

Library of Congress Control Number: 2023924538

First edition

For Jim
Cheers to twenty years, my love.

Chapter 1

The searing August sun had finally relented, sinking toward a brief rest on the horizon before its nightly free fall. Another day in Fort Myers was ending right along with Belle Carson's chores. The twenty-seven-year-old had finished yanking weeds and turning soil in one of several gardens she cared for along the Caloosahatchee River. The strenuous work left her dirty, tired, and nearly always content. For her, gardening offered a unique blend of challenges and rewards that changed with, and were defined by, whatever season was ruling the calendar. Of late, southwest Florida's summer heat and soaking rain had sapped the flower beds of nutrients, leaving them starved for heaps of compost, which she'd provided by the shovelful.

Belle removed her soiled apron and headed across the sandy yard toward a small white cottage. Lifting her long chestnut-brown braid, she ran the apron across her damp neck, wondering if her usual visitors had arrived.

"There you are, little ones," she said softly, nearing the cottage.

This evening, a charm of goldfinches was once again feeding on thistles and teasels that grew along a side wall of the wooden structure. As Belle got closer, the birds flew off and regrouped in a nearby live oak tree, chattering nonstop. She dropped the apron on a step and walked up to the landing, where she began tending to her own plants, some on the porch floor, others atop citrus crates. Zebra longwings and bumblebees hovered over potted pentas, cornflowers, and verbena as she watered; Carolina jessamine vines hugged both porch posts. A leathery staghorn fern attached to a disk of cypress wood hung over the front door, its forked fronds mimicking deer antlers.

Belle had long adored collecting and nurturing all sorts of plants, and now, she was getting paid to do it. Last year, in 1888, she'd been hired by Mina Edison, wife of world-renowned inventor Thomas Edison, to create several gardens on the couple's expansive winter estate. As if digging in such notable dirt was not an enticing enough prospect, the coveted position also included lodgings in the charming cottage next door.

The Edisons' purchase of their thirteen-acre tract four years earlier had been an astounding development for Fort Myers, a sleepy cow town on Florida's less-developed Gulf Coast. Suddenly, a community of 375 residents was being noted around the world in newspaper reports that highlighted Edison's plans for both a cold-weather retreat and a well-equipped workspace. The editor of the local *Fort Myers Press* fed the town's hunger to celebrate with capital letters and an extra helping of ink.

The great electrician, after a thorough look over the entire state, has chosen FORT MYERS as his WINTER HOME and has erected a LABORATORY nearby to carry out his experiments!

With more than six hundred U.S. patents to his name, the internationally recognized businessman was transforming the country and the world. He—or rather, his wife—had changed Belle's world, too, by giving her the chance to work for and live next door to the Edison family. After enduring years of a tormented childhood, then living a safe but sheltered existence as a young woman, Belle had finally begun to develop meaningful friendships and had even opened her heart to romance. The past year had truly blessed her with an abundance of good fortune, including a place of her own.

The square one-room cottage was simple but cozy. Belle had stitched together cotton flour bags for curtains and had sewn a gingham pillow for the rocking chair. Coffee cans filled with flowers topped every surface, including her dresser and a small table reserved for a tin washbasin. An elegant gateleg table was the finest piece in the room, its hinged legs carved in a reeded pattern. Her shell-pink bedspread and a river view added to the homespun charm.

The small, quaint house was located just beyond the Edisons' property line on the grounds of Baker's Boarding, a long-established business that was constantly bustling with travelers, mostly northerners who flocked to Fort Myers to bask in its subtropical climes. Baker's sparkling reputation for top-notch lodging and food was well earned, and its hardworking owner Abigail Baker was determined to maintain it. From the time Belle was a teenager, she'd considered Abigail family. Now, as an adult, Belle was even closer to her, in all ways.

"Goodness," she said, waving her hands back and forth inside the stuffy cottage.

She parted the curtains and inched up both windows, hoping to stir up the muggy air languishing inside. Through the glass, she spotted her sweetheart, Boone Larkin, next door at the Edison estate, where he worked, too. He'd been elsewhere when she arrived home at the cottage, but now she could see him and hear the thud of his sledgehammer as he drove in wooden posts for a new fence that would run between Baker's and the Edison property. Years of blazing sun and drenching rain had deteriorated the original barrier.

Boone had moved to Fort Myers in 1885 to work with the original crew Edison hired to build his laboratory and a pair of identical homes known collectively as Seminole Lodge, an homage to the rich history of the Seminole Indian tribe in southwest Florida. Now, four years later, Boone served as the Edisons' full-time carpenter, painter, and all-around fix-it man and lived aboard his sailboat anchored in the Caloosahatchee. Both his and Belle's jobs were important because the Edisons, especially when in New Jersey as they were now, wanted their property and their reputation as good neighbors to be well maintained.

Belle watched as Boone dug what looked to be the final posthole, his dungarees smudged with sand and black ash from burning the old posts. As the evening sky began to welcome twilight, she could still detect a crescent of golden curls bouncing beneath his straw hat with each jab he took at the ground. She'd met him last year when she was hired by the Edisons, and a casual friendship between them had developed. Then, following an exchange of deeply personal secrets, they'd begun to explore a romantic relationship, and in recent months had even talked of marriage.

Smoothing one curtain's curled hem, Belle recalled that night. Under a new moon, Boone had kissed her ring finger as they floated the river on his boat, the water's black surface seeming to sparkle with stars. He'd made it clear that he wanted a family, especially since he was estranged from his kin in central Florida. And despite her troublesome upbringing, she'd agreed—with a surprising measure of confidence—to having children in the future. She thought perhaps she would fare well as a mother, even thrive, like resilient candy-tuft growing in the narrow gaps of a stone wall.

Now she watched as Boone laid down his shovel and turned away from her, walking in the opposite direction toward a stack of hand tools—moving, as always, with a slight limp. He'd endured his share of hardship, too. But now, together, their future seemed as sure and sweet as the town's summer mango crop.

Suddenly, Belle spotted a shadowy figure walking briskly en route to the Edison property. *Here we go,* she thought. Occasionally, a curious boarder from Baker's would wander over to Seminole Lodge, undeterred by the fence. Abigail, Boone, or Belle would kindly but firmly stop the would-be trespasser, the three of them fiercely protective of the estate. Belle knew that right now Abigail was probably busy serving dessert, so she grabbed a candle stuck to a pie pan and left the cottage. She hurried down the porch steps and rounded the corner in the direction of the Lodge.

"Hello? May I help you?" Belle asked loudly, into the night. She scurried toward what appeared to be a female figure heading onto the property. "Excuse me, ma'am, but the Edisons aren't here and their estate is private." She quickly caught up to the person, who'd abruptly stopped.

"Did you just call me *ma'am*?" The woman squinted at Belle. She had a scarf tied around her face like a bandit, a flawed defense against pesky mosquitoes that visitors to the area often employed. Belle noted that the scarf was quite pretty, adorned with colorful birds. "I'll have you know that I am young and vital," the woman hissed. She yanked down the scarf as if to prove it.

Belle thought the woman was indeed attractive, but at that moment her face looked rather ghoulish in the candlelight. "My apologies, Miss . . ."

"*Mrs.* Smeltzer . . . ," the woman snapped.

"I'm sorry, Mrs. Smeltzer, it's just that we keep close watch over the Edison homes. We try to be good neighbors while they're away."

The woman looked Belle up and down in the flickering light. "Seems to me, instead of sticking your nose into other people's business, you should be washing the dirt off of it."

Belle reached up and wiped at the tip of her nose, which was probably smeared with soil. "Please go back to Baker's," she said. "I assume you're staying there?"

"I'll do as I wish," the woman said. She stayed put for a moment, then huffed, twirled away from Belle, and began walking back toward the boardinghouse.

Belle watched this Mrs. Smeltzer without concern. Even if the boarder complained about the talking-to Belle had given her, unflappable Abigail would have no trouble managing the curt woman.

She reentered the cottage and filled the round basin with water, then washed and toweled off. When she was done, she crossed the room. As she passed by the narrow bed, she ran her palm across the length of her cat, stretched out on the thin coverlet.

"Not a care in the world, eh, Coquina?" she said. The brown tabby purred.

The truth was, Belle couldn't say the same about herself at that very moment. She walked to the dresser and grabbed the knobs of its top drawer. With a yank, she opened it and pulled out a black dress for tomorrow's funeral.

• • •

The Fort Myers cemetery was tucked away due northwest of Front Street, the town's main hub. Billy's Creek bubbled along one side, populated by green herons that appeared to tiptoe through the water that bordered such hallowed ground.

Visitors to the peaceful cemetery were not always mourners, especially during summer months when several Chickasaw plum trees growing among the headstones bore fruit. Townsfolk knelt beneath the trees, not to pray, but to quietly collect yellow plums to eat fresh or boil into a tangy jelly.

This morning, the cemetery was crowded because of the funeral for Betsy Carson, Belle's adoptive mother. The service, nearly over, had been brief in part because every other Carson was either known to be dead or suspected of having died. The town's pastor had offered Belle the opportunity to speak about Betsy, but she'd declined. She may have shared the Carsons' surname, but she didn't share their blood, and she had no desire to be defined as a family member.

From her seat in the second row next to Boone, Belle could see a freshly dug grave between a headstone that read "Nelson Carson"—for her adoptive father—and a small sandstone marker for Benjamin Carson, the baby boy who'd drowned a year before Belle was adopted. She noted the absence of a marker for the Carsons' grown son, Julius, who'd disappeared last year and was presumed drowned. *Good,* she thought. *Remain erased.* Only she and Boone knew exactly how her ghastly adoptive brother had died and where he'd sunk before the devil yanked him down the rest of the way to where he belonged. When a small shudder crept up her back, Boone's hand instantly touched it. He mouthed, "You all right?" She nodded and offered a faint smile. Behind them she heard Jed Jenkins murmuring to Clay Dawson, the town's cabinetmaker.

"That's a fine toe pincher, Clay," Jed said, referring to Betsy's coffin.

Clay had built it wide at the top and tapered at the toe end, wasting no space. Jed's comment reminded Belle that no one really knew what to say at funerals, especially this one. Few people were as unremarkable as Betsy.

Poor Clay, Belle thought. Last year, he'd built coffins for his brother and sister-in-law who died from the same illness, leaving their adolescent daughters orphaned. Belle knew the road ahead would be hard for the girls; her own mother had died giving birth to her. But, unlike Belle in her early years, these girls were well cared for by Clay and his kind sister.

A ginger-haired woman sitting beside Belle said to her softly, "I didn't think I'd see you here."

Belle remained staring straight ahead. "I'm here for our town, Etta . . . our rituals."

Etta tsk-tsked. "What kind of a parent allows someone else to raise their child? Shameful. I mean no disrespect to your father, but what a sad excuse for a mother."

Stiffening, Belle took a deep breath. Betsy—a sad excuse for a mother indeed.

After Belle's mother, Eva, died, Betsy and Nelson Carson had adopted her as a newborn, a "replacement" for their own baby who'd drowned. The substitution turned out to be a failed experiment for everyone; no one was served by it. To young Belle, Betsy had seemed unaware that she was a mother at all. The more apt term for her might have been *a fly on the wall.* Every now and then, Betsy's small head would twist around to catch a glimpse of something moving in her house, but then she'd return to whatever else was holding her attention, which was not raising children. From the beginning, Betsy's husband, Nelson, favored Julius and seemed oblivious to how vulnerable Belle was to his son's unspeakable cruelty. Maybe Nelson had been blinded by the fog that seemed to swirl around his wife, or maybe he'd been drowning in anger at her for losing track of their baby along the creek. Either way, the result was the same: no one saw Belle.

Finally, at fourteen, she'd run away to Merle Duggan's general store following a violent scuffle with Julius. Merle took her in, protected her, and raised her with the help of his dear friend, Abigail Baker, who visited often. Thankfully, the

Carsons made no attempts to take her back. In the years after Belle had moved into Duggan's, she'd never asked Merle or Abigail whether her switching families had prompted rumors, but she was sure there must have been plenty. The town might not yet have electricity like Mr. Edison had promised it one day would, but gossip pulsed through its streets with comparable voltage.

Belle's new life at Duggan's had unfolded slowly and soundly, as Merle and Abigail eased her into existence. She'd come to them as a cloudy droplet of water, but over time the light from the loving pair revealed that she'd become a rainbow, her colors arching taller and wider as her personality developed. The first to recognize her interest in plants, Abigail had walked Belle to Baileys' Nursery, where Gus and Grace Bailey plied her with as much information about gardening as a teenager could soak up. Botany became a common language between Belle and the caring couple, their friendship another reliable relationship in Belle's life. Before long, she was riding around town aboard her adult treadle tricycle—a gift from Merle—tending to neighbors' gardens, accepting only waves of gratitude or the occasional jar of honey or pickled peppers. After the dozen years she'd spent with Merle and Abigail, she'd grown into a woman who was open to exploring relationships and opportunities, the very woman who'd interviewed for the Edison job. Landing the position, moving out of Duggan's, organizing a local women's club, and meeting Boone had all deepened her confidence.

Now, one last reminder of those darker years was gone. Betsy Carson had been found by neighbors several days ago inside her house. Her body was on the floor, her head resting in the fireplace, eyes staring up into the flue—as odd in death as she was in life.

"Good riddance," Belle whispered.

A blue jay screeched somewhere along the edge of the

cemetery as several men lowered the wooden coffin into the ground. Pastor Mitchell Peck opened his Bible and read a passage that several attendees recognized and softly recited with him.

Belle tried to focus on all the good new things in her life: lush gardens, cozy lodgings, first love. Still, she couldn't help but worry that her past would keep her from one more thing she wanted to experience. And so, when she heard Pastor Peck say, "Let us pray," Belle obeyed and sent up a plea to God.

Please give me a second chance.

Chapter 2

Belle had insisted to Merle that only she and Boone should attend Betsy's funeral since he had so much work to do that day, and she'd promised that if anyone asked why he and Abigail weren't at the cemetery, she'd mention the sheriff's need for help. And so, he and the woman he loved were spending the morning at Duggan's. Merle was in the storage room, clearing a space to accommodate the lawman's request. Abigail was out in the store's public area, gathering supplies for her boarding-house kitchen.

"If I'd had to predict which of my friends would shoot a man, I'd have put money on Poppy," Merle heard Abigail say from the next room. "Never Amelia."

Poppy Peck was married to the town's Methodist pastor, Mitchell, who last year had been caught kissing a parishioner in the church's bell tower. Amelia Polk, who couldn't see well enough to catch anybody kissing anyone, ran the community's apothecary.

"Amelia didn't shoot anyone," Merle called back loudly, his deep voice booming. "She just grazed him." He carefully straightened his considerable stock of glass pickle jars that he'd just restacked in one corner. "Why would you peg Poppy as a gunslinger?"

Abigail stuck her head into the storage room. "No need to shout. I can hear you just fine, Squirrel," she said, calling him by his nickname. Merle was constantly foraging for merchandise to meet his customers' every need. With one hand resting on her ample waist, Abigail then replied to his earlier question. "After what Mitchell did, I wouldn't blame Poppy for wanting to give him a little lead poisoning."

Merle chuckled and began stacking bolts of butcher paper to look like firewood. "Now, now, those two are working things out. Let's not have Poppy shooting Pastor Peck."

Abigail walked back into the main room of the store. Duggan's was the oldest structure on Front Street, and one of its walls still had a mail slot carved into it from when Merle served as the region's postmaster.

Not even a minute passed before she poked her head back around the doorway and aimed a banana at Merle's pickle supply, one eye squinted shut. "When does our shooter arrive?"

"I'm not sure, honey. Sheriff Clark said he'll drop her off soon and then prepare for his sail to Key West."

Abigail disappeared once more. Merle heard creaking noises as she made her way back to the produce section, where the floorboards were loose.

"Whenever our jailbird arrives, we'll be ready for her," he called out.

He guessed that Abigail had stopped near the produce bins and was sampling grapes in the way she usually did. He let his imagination linger on that image, her stout body wrapped in a form-fitting apron she wore over a long, pale-blue dress that matched her eyes.

"Well, I know Sheriff Clark appreciates your help," he heard her say. "This way, he can take that sticky-fingered hoodlum to jail down in the Keys, and our Amelia can serve her time right here . . . in Duggan's Dungeon."

Just like Abigail with Baker's, Amelia was devoted to her apothecary business and took abundant pride in serving her customers. Crime in Fort Myers was generally limited to the occasional fruit thief or drunken cow hunters coming to blows, so—according to Amelia—she'd been taken aback recently when a box of nerve and bone liniment went missing from her store. Next, all her Caswell-Massey cologne disappeared. When Amelia finally spotted a man attempting to steal a bottle of laudanum, she'd snapped and reached for a gun.

"Good progress," Merle said quietly to himself. Finished with arranging the butcher paper, he moved to the storeroom door and peered out. Abigail was indeed standing close to the fruit, just where he'd pictured her. An orchard basket full of bumpy baking potatoes sat on the floor next to her. "Amelia's going to be just fine, dear."

"Well, I feel terrible that I didn't give that marauder the boot from Baker's," Abigail said as she pressed a pineapple against her nose and took a whiff. "I'm quite good at reading my boarders, but this one was smooth. He even gathered eggs for me every morning of his stay."

Merle raised an eyebrow at her. "Six for you, a dozen for him?"

Abigail waved him off with one hand but smiled. "I just hate that I may be losing my touch. And poor Amelia. Because of me, she's landed in the pokey."

A mere four foot eleven, Amelia had confessed to the sheriff that because she was fed up with her pharmacy being robbed by the thief, she'd grabbed her late mother's Colt single-action snub-nosed revolver and fired it right at him. Or so she thought. Wearing a new pair of thick eyeglasses, she'd taken aim several inches off target and the bullet only sideswiped the man's left shoulder.

Following the arrest, Sheriff Frederick Clark reported that a bulge noted in the region of the suspect's manhood had turned out to be several bottles of chloral hydrate, a sedative. The rest of the merchandise taken during the weeklong stealing spree was later confiscated from under the mattress in his room at Baker's.

Because Fort Myers had yet to build a jail, suspects arrested in Lee County were transported south for detention in Key West. But since Amelia was a long-established business owner and respected citizen, Sheriff Clark had decided not to formally charge her. He had, however, asked Merle if he'd keep the harmless gunslinger "in custody" for a few days, to send a message to others who might consider vigilante justice. Merle had agreed, grinning right along with the sheriff as they'd discussed the arrangement. Duggan's tidy nook would make a fine cell, a rope across the door enough to contain the ninety-five-pound, nearly blind Amelia.

Merle crossed the room to Abigail. His tall, lanky body towered over hers. He placed his large hands on both her shoulders and kissed her forehead. "No one got seriously hurt, honey, and now the word on the street is 'Don't mess with Amelia.'" He bent his knees just enough to be eye level with Abigail. "And you haven't lost your touch. Not with me anyway." He gave her a wink.

•••

Abigail and Merle had been friends for many years, sharing a penchant for business—and more importantly—a love for Belle, which grew each year they parented her. Merle had always called Abigail "my gal," but over the years, she'd shied away from any hint of romance with him. She couldn't face losing him as a friend if love didn't suit them. But last fall, when Merle asked Abigail to consider reimagining their relationship, she'd agreed. Perhaps it was watching Belle and Boone fall in love that had lowered her guard. Or maybe, as she and Merle moved through their fifties, she'd realized their time to be together—fully together—was short. Whatever had compelled her to open her heart, the experience so far was as fulfilling as their platonic friendship had been. They still lived separately—she at Baker's and he at Duggan's—but only a mile lay between them. Now, with Belle living on the Baker property, Merle visited often and even stayed some nights at Baker's. Boarders assumed Merle worked at the establishment because he often did, right along with Boone, helping Abigail with whatever she needed. Both men ate well in return.

"Come see what I've done," Merle said. He led Abigail to the storage area.

Together they surveyed the small room. It was still crammed with sacks of coffee beans, canned goods, and puncheons filled with kerosene. But in the last hour, Merle had piled provisions up to the ceiling, creating a sufficient rectangle in the interior. He'd fluffed up the single bed Belle had slept on when she lived there, and the striped curtain she'd sewn still hung over a small window on the north wall. Merle's stacked butcher paper "fire" gave the room a cozy feel, as did potted herbs he'd brought in from the porch. The bed was draped with a soft spread, and the aroma of coffee beans was pleasant, not overbearing.

"How's it look, my gal?" Merle asked, twirling a chubby cigar tucked in his breast pocket.

Abigail eyed the revamped space while patting the bun atop her head as if it were a well-behaved child.

"Well, it looks more like a hotel room than a prison cell." She turned and gave Merle's arm a peck, kissing his shirtsleeve. "Good work, Warden."

Chapter 3

The August weather so far had been typical—hot and rainy, the bright summer sun frequently humbled by thick gray clouds that managed to obscure it. Boone's shirt was soaked with a mix of sweat and light drizzle as he worked on the final stretch of the Edisons' new fence. As he nailed a picket into the top rail, he saw Norville Decker striding toward him from the caretaker's cottage, the only original structure on the property. Decker was a crusty northerner who'd moved to southwest Florida seemingly determined to dismiss anything positive the exotic region had to offer. Nothing suited the caretaker. The fragrant plants were too *smelly*. The abundant sunshine was *glaring*. Even the exquisite silver-scaled tarpon were *prehistoric monsters*. Norville Decker was inherently negative, but somehow Boone liked him; maybe because he thought the wiry, nervous man could use someone on his side.

"Well, he's gone and done it again," Decker fumed, waving a piece of paper in the air, then quickly tucking it into his pants pocket to protect it from the mist.

"Good morning to you, too," Boone said, manhandling a thick post to check its sturdiness.

"The Edisons have invited a visitor to the Lodge," Decker said, sounding annoyed.

Boone raised his eyebrows. "Well, doggone. It's as if they own the place."

Decker dismissed the comment and continued to gripe. "It's some Virginia woman."

Boone wiped away a drip clinging to his eyebrow. "Who do they know in Virginia?"

Decker looked up at the gray sky for a moment and shook his head, as if Boone had asked a ridiculous question. "Her *name* is Virginia. Virginia P. Moore. She's apparently from Tennessee, but the Edisons know her because she spends part of her summer at that . . . Chautauqua Institution." Decker tilted his head back and forth, the quail-like tuft of hair atop it swaying back and forth. "Hoity-toity . . ."

Boone had no idea what Decker was going on about, so he got down to business. "Exactly what can I do to make her happy and make you stop whining?"

Decker narrowed his already small eyes. "Watch your tone, boy. Finish the fence and then start working on boxes for every window of the Lodge." He placed one palm over his heart and batted his lashless eyelids. "Is your beloved ready to plant her pretty flowers?"

Boone tapped the face of his hammer on his palm. "Of course. Belle's always three steps ahead of us both, and you know it."

Decker grinned, accentuating his mole-like muzzle of a nose. He seemed to enjoy teasing Boone about his having fallen for the girl next door. Still, Boone knew Decker considered Belle a worthy coworker. One morning, in his gruff way, Decker had complimented her, saying to Boone, "That petite thing works like the dog that you are." That was as close to eloquence as the northern transplant came.

As Decker rambled on about Miss Moore's visit, Boone's

thoughts turned to Belle. He pictured her wearing that signature straw hat of hers, covered in colorful fishing lures. Shortly after they met, she'd shared with him that she'd begun collecting lost lures during her bleak childhood, something pretty to call her own.

Boone had certainly found *her* pretty. But when Belle moved in next door, he was still denying himself anything pleasurable, especially the company of women. He knew he didn't deserve any indulgences after making a deadly mistake back home. Yet he was instantly drawn to Belle, her quiet way a welcome relief from the constant noise in his life—tools striking and sawing, Decker's endless droning, the nagging guilt rattling around his soul. He'd craved more silence in his life, and this gentle woman drew him in with her serenity, not to mention those deep-brown eyes and ample lips. Now, life without Belle seemed unimaginable. They were clearly a couple, the word *our* a regular part of their conversations. *Look! It's* our *smiling moon. Abigail's making* our *favorite soup. Our owl is back in his hollow.* Marriage seemed like a solid next step, followed by children. But regrettably, there was family trouble in Kissimmee.

Decker's sneezes, frequent and sloppy, brought Boone back to their conversation. Wiping a sleeve across his pointy sunburned nose, Decker doled out tasks.

"Fence, flower boxes, porch sweeping," he said, using his long, spindly fingers to tick them off. "Miss Moore will spend three days here. She'll walk the grounds, but no one but family stays in the Lodge, so she'll be given the finest room at Baker's." Decker's face soured. "And by that, I mean the one with the fewest mice."

"All right, enough, Decker," Boone said. Abigail and Decker were much like the stuff of Edison and Nikola Tesla's highly publicized War of the Currents, their opposite energies creating constant friction. "Go add up some numbers or something. Let me do the heavy lifting, as usual."

Decker grunted and walked away, mumbling to himself. As Boone returned his focus to the project before him, his mind drifted back to his earlier thoughts. Maybe it was finally time for him to try to mend yet another fence.

The one standing between him and his family.

Chapter 4

Both Belle and Boone had been busy for the past two days, sprucing up the Lodge for the Edisons' visitor who'd arrive that night. Still, Belle had managed to make time for friends, who were sitting with her now.

"Let's start passing around snacks," she suggested, and reached for a plate of biscuits stuffed with ham salad lying on a nearby table.

Last year, she'd formed a women's group called the Circle Club. Their activities had thus far consisted of organizing community repair projects and offering emotional and practical support to each other whenever it was needed. No larger mission had been established, and no specific schedule existed for when to hold meetings. Members simply looked forward to seeing one another and gathered as often as possible, in whatever location was available and convenient. Belle was thrilled that in just over a year, a tight bond had developed between her and these seven interesting and caring people. She'd originally reached out to the women to bolster herself, to develop relationships beyond her most precious ones with Merle and

Abigail. Now Belle was delighted to call each of the ladies a dear friend.

This afternoon, their chairs were arranged in a circle—hence the club's name—on the second floor of the town's real estate and loan office. The space also served as a temporary courthouse until one could be built, and land agent C. J. Huelsenkamp was expert at leveraging his access to potential buyers who were sometimes above him. Banners featuring phrases like "Fine farms & orange groves—buy now!" and "A grand future predicted for Caloosahatchee country!" hung on every wall. The ladies, however, were not in the market for land. They were focused instead on ham salad sandwiches and a pitcher of sweet tea. Abigail prepared refreshments for every meeting, too busy at Baker's to attend any of them, but committed to feeding her fellow club members. Today, an empty chair in the circle served as a reminder that one woman who did always attend was absent.

"Abigail makes the best buttermilk biscuits," Sadie Tillis said, holding a sandwich in her left hand. Her other was patting the back of a newborn cradled against her engorged breasts. One of the town's two wet nurses, Sadie, was an enthusiastic club member. With five young children of her own at home, she saw meetings as a way to escape her *little hellions* for an hour.

Paulette York dabbed at the corners of her tinted lips with a napkin. "I need to learn some cooking tips from Abigail," she said, inspecting her sandwich. "As they say, the way to a man's heart is through his stomach."

Alice Bishop raked her fingers through her short hair. "Sounds like a very gruesome path to the heart . . ."

Paulette smiled and shrugged her slight shoulders. Tall and graceful, she was well known in town for her history of sporadic relationships—even engagements. She'd recently begun spending time with Duke Davis, the town's blacksmith. A former Miss Tampa, Paulette was striking, her long glossy hair nearly as red as the glowing coals in Duke's forge. Any cooking skills Paulette gained would simply sweeten a pot already brimming with honey.

Nearly as lovely was Hazel Cravin, whose parents owned the general store that rivaled Duggan's. Cravin & Company had somehow scored a coveted tie to the Edisons, one that had them regularly shipping fruit from local groves to the family's home in West Orange, New Jersey. Hazel's mother, Ida, was one of the least-liked people in town—bossy, self-righteous, and desperate to become friends with Mina Edison.

It was obvious to everyone in town that Ida loved playing lead hen, especially when it came to her only child. Before Hazel became a member of the club, she'd been smothered by her mother's controlling ways, never allowed to express her opinions or desires. The "perfect" daughter, Hazel had been raised to play second fiddle to everyone, especially her mother. But, to Ida's horror, Hazel had joined the Circle Club, found her voice, and was now even working outside the home.

"Food may be the way to a man's heart," Hazel said, grinning, "but surely after marriage we need to stay as busy in the boudoir as we do in the kitchen, right, ladies?"

The club's youngest member at twenty, Alice rolled her eyes but also blushed.

"Oh, Lord," Sadie said, shaking her head. "The only thing I want to stay busy at in the bedroom is . . ." She closed her eyes and pretended to snore. The women chuckled, but Belle knew the topic might be awkward for Poppy, considering her husband's dalliance in the bell tower. She changed the subject.

"So, our empty chair," she said, pointing to it. "As you know, Amelia has begun her several-day lockup."

Poppy opened her ever-present Bible to a page marked with a palmetto spear. "'Fear thou not; for I *am* with thee: be not dismayed; for I *am* thy God: I will strengthen thee; yea, I will help thee; yea, I will uphold thee with the right hand of my righteousness.'" She looked up from the page.

"Amelia's in Duggan's, not hell, right?" Alice deadpanned, crossing one alligator-skin boot over the other. Her father ran the local taxidermy shop.

Belle smiled. "Hazel has kindly stepped in to help at the drugstore in Amelia's absence." She looked over at Hazel. "How are you finding the work?"

Hazel yanked on a long blonde curl and released it, the silky hair bouncing back up. "Interesting, exciting, fulfilling— everything my mother would hate to hear." Her face lit up. "John's offered to help me at Polk's whenever he can slip away from the grove."

Last year, Hazel had gotten smacked in the mouth by a tipped ball during the club's attempt to play baseball, a plan Ida caught wind of before marching over to where the "game" was underway. When John Parker had comforted the in- jured Hazel and then asked permission—right in front of her mother—to court her, Ida had nearly fainted from anger! Not only was her daughter playing a man's sport, but Hazel had also been rewarded for doing so with attention from one of the well-to-do Parkers, the prominent family that owned a large grapefruit grove.

Belle had truly enjoyed witnessing Ida's histrionics; the woman just got under her skin. One of the worst things about Ida was her indulgent, despicable love affair with elaborate picture hats festooned with long, garish feathers. The preten- tious woman supported the Women's Christian Temperance Movement and *abstinence from all things harmful*, yet her fondness for trendy hats supported the slaughter of millions of herons, flamingos, and roseate spoonbills. Each year, countless plume birds were killed by hunters so fashion heathens like Ida could feed their outlandish fetish. It was clear to Belle that using brightly colored, artfully crafted fishing lures was a far more compassionate choice. Also clear—at least to her—was that some of Ida's very worst qualities weren't as easily noted as her gaudy hats.

"When Amelia returns to her store," Poppy asked Hazel, "will you stay on at Polk's?"

"I hope to," Hazel said, watching a mint leaf circling her tea as she swirled the glass.

"How *about* our sassy Amelia!" Sadie said. "I can picture her wielding a crochet needle or two, but whipping out that 'storekeeper's friend'?" Sadie turned her head away from the baby and whooped.

Alice agreed with a snort and wiped biscuit crumbs off her pants. "That crook's lucky Amelia's got eyes like a possum."

Belle laughed and scanned the notes in her lap. "We plan to hold our next meeting inside Duggan's so we can include Amelia. All in favor?"

Everyone raised their hands. When Poppy kept hers up, Belle called on her.

"I've got an update on my new granddaughter," she said, beaming. "Little Sarah is healthy, as is our daughter. And thank you for your offer, Sadie, but everything is . . . flowing nicely."

The women conveyed their warm congratulations, talking over one another. Belle added hers, wondering if God would ever answer her recent prayer—that one day, she and Boone would have a child of their own.

Just then, the bell on the Methodist church rang twice. Paulette flashed a beauty-queen smile, her emerald eyes sparkling. "The sound of success, ladies."

Organizing a group of handymen to repair the busted bell had been the club's first project.

"That lovely sound also means the meeting is over," Belle announced. "As always, thank you all for coming."

"Can I bring Coconut to Duggan's?" Alice asked. She finally owned a real animal—a dog—and was no longer carting around odd stuffed specimens from her father's "botched" taxidermy collection. Because Alice was considered odd by many in town, Belle had invited her to join the club. As she'd suspected, Alice had instead proved to be funny, kind, and refreshingly independent.

Belle surveyed the members, who were all nodding enthusiastically, likely relieved to lay eyes on a dog instead of atrocities like the head of a flamingo sewn onto the body of a river otter.

"So, we all agree." Belle scribbled Coconut's name in her notes. "I think Amelia will approve, too."

And with that, the women began to return the chairs to their original spots, including the one they'd set out in honor of their strong-willed, weak-eyed friend.

Chapter 5

Boone began the morning after Miss Moore's arrival by skimming the newspaper on the deck of his boat. He had to hand it to Stephen Fitzgerald, editor of the *Press*: Fitz knew that any particulars about the Edisons sold papers. As a result, he frequently rewrote stories that first appeared in national and international papers. He did his best to make the story read as if he'd just chatted with someone close to the famous family, using phrases like, "We've just learned . . ."

> We've just learned that the tireless inventor refers to himself as a "two-shift man" and works sixteen out of every twenty-four hours.

Fitz would also buff up the facts from time to time and had even used the phrase *elegant yacht* to describe the rickety fishing sloop that originally transported Edison to Fort Myers. Fitz knew as well that readers were always eager for updates on an exciting pledge Edison had made four years ago to light up the town. Once, at a community gathering, the inventor had fired up multiple chandelier-style electroliers inside his home, the glowing Seminole Lodge a reminder to townsfolk that they, too, might one day enjoy electricity. While most residents were eager for Edison to illuminate Fort Myers, several families were concerned that lights would keep their cows and chickens awake at night and were against the project. Others were convinced Edison's apparatus would blow up the city.

All the gear needed—a powerful dynamo, lamps, wires—had already been shipped in, and poles had been erected along Front Street. Oscar Powell, the town's telegraph operator, learned how to equip the poles during the Edisons' honeymoon stay. Recently, volunteers nicknamed the Lamplighters had run underground cables along the one-mile stretch from the laboratory to the downtown gear. The town's main street was rumored to be the first step toward eventually replacing tallow candles and kerosene lamps in every home and business. But, as of now, the most important piece of equipment— the dynamo that converted mechanical rotation into electric power—was collecting dust in Edison's laboratory.

Boone set down his empty coffee cup on the boat's deck and continued reading the *Press*. This morning Fitz had included a tidbit he knew the locals would gobble up like fried potatoes.

> We've just learned that our dear
> neighbor Mrs. Mina Edison is quite
> busy this summer caring for the
> Edisons' darling one-year-old daughter
> Madeline, born last May in Glenmont,
> the sprawling New Jersey estate Mr.
> Edison purchased for his bride. The
> little girl is affectionately referred to
> as Toots by relatives—yet another
> adorable nickname! As you may recall
> from previous reports, two of Edison's

children from his first marriage are
otherwise known as Dot and Dash, a
reference to his work with Morse code
as a brass pounder during and after
the Civil War.

Because traveling south was a long and wearisome journey via water and rail, the chances of an Edison visit this winter were slim, especially considering Toots was still an infant. The extended family hadn't stayed at the riverside estate for three years now, small children and big business always getting in the way. Rumor had it that Edison was pursuing a renewed interest in producing refined ore, and some reports claimed he was overseeing operations in New Jersey at one of the largest ore-crushing mills in the world. Still, the *Press* constantly stoked hope that a glimpse of the famous family was right around the corner. Boone read the latest claim.

A WINTER SOJOURN BY OUR DISTINGUISHED NEIGHBORS AWAITS! SUNSHINE MAY BRING BOTH THE EDISONS AND ELECTRICITY TO FORT MYERS!

The story then referenced Edison's respiratory issues—yet again—and suggested southwest Florida's juicy, tropical climate would serve as ideal "salve for his lungs." But, despite the inked optimism, behind closed doors and even around the bar at Billy's Saloon, many folks agreed that neither the Edisons nor electricity was likely to arrive this winter.

"One day, Fitz," Boone said.

Skimming the rest of the page, he noted the announcement of a visit by the woman he was about to meet, Virginia P. Moore.

MINA'S CHUM TO DROP IN.

As a pair of leggy sandhill cranes glided overhead, Boone wondered if plucky ol' Fitz would land an interview with her.

...

While walking from his boat down the long wharf toward the Edison property, Boone noticed Decker standing next to a woman who was taller and thicker than the slight caretaker. She was full-figured and seemingly overdressed for a stroll around thirteen acres.

Boone joined the pair just as Decker was saying, "And we can tour both houses, too." He swept his arm across the air with a dramatic flourish toward the butter-yellow homes as if presenting a jewelry collection.

Acknowledging Decker with a raised eyebrow, Boone reached out a hand to their guest. "Welcome, Miss Moore. I'm Boone Larkin."

She smiled and offered him her bent hand. "Please, call me Virginia."

Decker inched a little closer to the woman and pointed both hands—as if aiming two revolvers—toward the perfectly flat river. "As you can see, Virginia, I ironed the water for you this morning." He flashed a rare smile, revealing his tiny square teeth, each one stained yellow from cigar smoke.

Boone craned his neck around to look at the Caloosahatchee, which was indeed a smooth sheet. Decker, waxing poetic? This was fresh ground.

"It's just lovely, Norville," she said, then glanced down at a hunter-case pocket watch she'd pulled out from her long coat. "Gentlemen, thank you in advance for your time, but let's not waste any more of it, agreed?" she said, her tone light. Boone eyed the overstuffed purse hanging from her arm. Apparently, she was a stickler for time but not for judicious packing. "Shall we?" She snapped the watch's lid shut.

Decker continued his odd behavior, slipping a scrawny arm through Virginia's. "Off we go, madam," he said, leading her in the direction of the two homes.

Boone stayed put, shocked that Virginia had allowed the bold move. He watched them walk arm in arm past the wind pump. Virginia didn't even flinch as her quirky host sneezed into the crook of his elbow. Was Decker in fact a charmer, somehow attractive to women with his rail-thin build, sunken sunburned cheeks, and naked eyelids? Or was he perhaps still tipsy from a bender at Billy's? Mr. Edison had, after all, just sent Decker a large chunk of back pay. Boone sighed and scratched his chin. Decker was now stroking the upright tuft of black hair in the middle of his bald head, and Virginia was chuckling at whatever he'd just said.

"I'll be damned," Boone said softly.

When the pair disappeared into one of the houses, Boone began work on the flower boxes he was building for nearly forty windows. So far, he'd completed a dozen. As he grabbed wood for the start of another, Belle approached from across the yard, pushing a wheelbarrow full of dirt. Despite her small frame, she handled the barrow as if it were filled with dead leaves, not a dense load of soil. He got up off his knees and walked over to her, smiling and happy, as he always was when she was headed his way.

When he first met Belle, Boone had kept his distance. But before long, he couldn't resist his desire to learn more about her, and a friendship soon developed. Then, one night, the intensity of their connection had exploded like an arrow off a bowstring. Belle had shown up at his boat, shaking and covered in blood. Together, they'd hurried by candlelight back to her cottage, where a man lay dead on the bed, a gaping hole in his neck. When Belle had explained that the doughy body was that of her childhood abuser—and that she'd fatally stabbed him—Boone had dragged the corpse to the riverbank and rolled it down into the blackness, where alligators might devour the evidence. That was only the first of several secrets they'd share over the course of their time spent together, each intimacy serving as wind in the sails of their fast-moving relationship.

"Good morning, sweetheart. I'll take that from here," he said, motioning toward the wheelbarrow. He kissed her lightly on the cheek, navigating his lips up and under the brim of her straw hat while holding his in place.

"Oh, I've got it," she said, "but thank you. And good morning." She swiped her sweaty chin across one cocked shoulder. "Already sticky out."

Boone walked beside her as she continued to push the wheelbarrow, a trowel stabbed in the mound of soil. He knew she was stubborn about pulling her own weight at work.

"Did you get a chance to meet Virginia Moore?" he asked, running a gloved hand across her back.

"Just briefly," she replied. "Abigail introduced me as she was loading up Miss Moore's purse with corn muffins, a jar of jam, and an orange. You know how she worries about anyone going hungry."

Boone chuckled. "So that's why Virginia's handbag is bursting at the seams."

They settled into their work areas in the Edisons' backyard, Boone hammering away while Belle squatted beside the completed boxes and scooped dirt into each one. After several minutes of silence, Boone asked, "How are you doing?"

Leveling the dirt inside one box, Belle said, "I can't go wrong with Abigail's amazing compost." A large mound on the Baker property held a rich mix of sawdust, coffee grounds, eggshells, horse manure, and chicken feathers.

"I mean *you*, Belle. Are you okay?" Boone asked. He pushed

up the brim of his straw hat to get a better look at her. "I mean with Betsy and all . . ."

Boone had been wondering if Betsy's death had created any angst for her. Yes, Belle had made it clear to him that the woman meant nothing to her, but loss was complicated. He knew firsthand that grief and anger could damage people and their relationships.

"I'm actually relieved," she answered, setting down her trowel and standing up. With her hands on her hips, she said, "It's strange how we don't realize how much is stewing inside of us until the lid gets lifted." She shrugged. "Betsy's death has done that for me. It's let what remained of my anger about the Carsons and Julius escape." She took a deep breath and exhaled. With a few steps, she was in front of him. She wiped soil off her palms and placed both hands on his chest. "I like this clean slate . . . for us," she said, looking up at him, her brown eyes focused on his lips.

He smiled and tipped back her hat. "Me too," he said, and then kissed her. As they drew apart, he told her, "I've been thinking about writing a letter to my parents."

Belle raised her eyebrows. "Some lid-lifting of your own?"

He shrugged one shoulder. "Maybe." He paused and then said, "*My* slate isn't clean, Belle."

She nodded and said softly, "I know. I absolutely hate what happened with your brother, but it was an accident. Surely your mother and father miss you after all this time."

Belle was right. It *had* been an accident, and telling her every detail had provided him with such relief. Still, he wasn't convinced his family missed him. Maybe they never even thought about him at all.

Boone had left behind his grieving family four years ago and joined the Edison construction crew. He'd never even heard of Fort Myers before departing Kissimmee, and he had known no one here—exactly the fresh start he was looking for. The mess he'd made involved his brother, Daniel, three years older with a build larger than Boone's but the same blue eyes and mop of sandy-blond curls. They'd always been close, riding side by side as cracker cowboys, moving cattle across fenceless wooded prairies. Together with their barking curs, they'd guided strays out from the thick underbrush, cracking braided leather whips atop their sure-footed horses. Daniel was a skilled cow hunter and an even better brother, loyal and protective. Then, one day, he was dead, and Boone himself was the one who'd—by mistake—done the killing.

Maybe he should have remained at home so his devastated mother and father could watch him suffer through intense guilt and pain. Truth was, he *had* stayed for a while, but the relationship with his parents was by then so fractured—surely the next thing in line to die—he'd thought it best for everyone that he simply disappear. So, leaving no word of his plan, he'd boarded a train to the Gulf Coast, resigning himself to a very different future: driving nails instead of cattle.

Boone chewed on his lower lip. "Do you think I should write to them?"

Belle stayed quiet for a moment and then answered. "Not everyone grows up in a loving family, Boone. I finally found mine, but you told me you've always had good folks." She smiled, revealing the small gap in her front teeth. "I think family is worth fighting for."

Boone reached up and cupped her cheek with his hand. "I'd be fighting for us, too . . . so we can start our life"—he paused, searching for words—"with as much wrangling done as possible."

Belle smiled. She wrapped her arms around his neck and hugged him. "I'm proud of you."

He hugged her back tightly and hoped that, somehow, he would find the words to begin to restore his family—if restoring it was even a possibility.

When they stood back from each other, Belle used both hands to right her tilted hat, the fishing lures falling back into place.

"Back to work for us," she said. "I've got to head over to Baileys' to pick up more plants." She grabbed the handle of a wagon, its wooden slats brushed with leftover yellow house paint. "I'd invite you, but you know how I tend to linger too long over there." She grinned.

"See you in a few days," he said in jest.

As she walked away, Boone resumed his work and began to consider the very best way to extend an olive branch northeast to Kissimmee.

• • •

When Virginia and Decker finally completed their tour of the homes and property, they approached Boone, who was organizing metal brackets into pairs.

"Boone, you and Norville have done a wonderful job keeping up the Edisons' estate," Virginia said, dabbing a lacy handkerchief across her brow. "Indoor plumbing, wire-mesh window screens." She refolded the square cloth. "Quite impressive."

"Thank you, Virginia," he said, examining her for a few seconds.

He noted that while her thin, straight lips made her appear serious-minded, Virginia's eyes twinkled as if she was ready for adventure. Studying her outfit, he could only imagine how overheated she must be. Her dark-brown duster featured decorative buttons that ran down one side of the coat and along both cuffs. A white ruffled collar poked out from a vest that led to a long skirt. Somehow, she'd navigated the yard sporting high-heeled, pointy black boots.

He nodded toward Decker. "Norville here does all the ironing, and I handle the rest."

Virginia smiled. "You two are a good team." She touched Decker's arm. "I'll tell Mina how well you took care of me."

Boone rolled his eyes as Virginia addressed her absurd tour guide.

"My pleasure, Virginia," Decker said, his deep bow causing his spectacles to slide down his nose, slippery with perspiration. Upon righting himself, he poked the thin bridge of his glasses, moving them back into place. "I'm off to wrestle numbers now," he said. "Perhaps I'll see you tomorrow?"

Virginia brushed off sand clinging to the fringe along the bottom of her purse. "Perhaps," she said, eyeing him up and down.

After Decker had moved out of earshot, Boone said, "Virginia, I think you cast some sort of"—he paused and wiggled his fingers beside each ear—"spell on Decker. He can be a little gloomy."

She chuckled. "Truly? Perhaps my positive attitude rubbed off on him. I do believe a sunny outlook is contagious." She popped open the pocket watch. "I suppose I'll wander back to Baker's for a nap," she said, fanning her face with her hand. "This heat has gotten the best of me."

Boone grinned. "And maybe Decker, too."

She hugged her fat purse to her body. "Oh, he's harmless . . . and quite amusing, in a wind-up toy sort of way."

Tired of discussing Decker, Boone asked, "Is there anything else I can help you with during your stay?"

Virginia pursed her lips together until they disappeared. "Well, as I shared with Norville, Mina encouraged my visit in the hopes that I might see a way to duplicate here the work I'm doing in Tennessee."

"I'm afraid I don't know anything about your work,

Virginia. The newspaper ran a brief story, but it just said you're a friend of Mina's, in town to look at property."

Virginia offered a dismissive wave of her hand. "Oh, I don't like reporters. They rarely let the facts derail a good story, so I fibbed about looking for acreage to Mr. . . . Fitz-something."

"Fitzgerald," Boone said. "So, why *are* you here?"

Her eyes sparkled. "Mina and I met several summers ago in New York. Her father, Lewis, cofounded the Chautauqua Institution, a lakeside camp formed for the education of Sunday school teachers." She explained that before long, the institute also began to offer a variety of programs to the public—performing arts, lectures, worship services, and recreational activities. "Mina and I"—she flicked open all ten fingers like exploding fireworks—"we just hit it off." She smiled. "We share a love for teaching and encouraging young women, so she was quite interested in my work promoting tomato clubs." Virginia stood a little straighter. "I'm Tennessee's first home demonstration agent."

Confused, Boone furrowed his eyebrows. "My sweetheart started a women's club here in town. Are tomato clubs . . . like that?"

"Well, I suppose, in a way. But our tomato clubs serve girls who live in rural areas. By growing and canning tomatoes, young ladies gain certain skills—everything from arithmetic to writing—which improve their confidence. They go on to host demonstrations for friends and family, and even enter competitions at county and state fairs." Little sparks seemed to alight from her brown eyes. "The prizes offered are pretty nifty, too."

Boone swatted away a wasp. "Well, Belle not only organized a club, she also gardens for the Edisons."

Virginia tilted her head. "I believe I met a Belle at Baker's. Is she *your* Belle?"

His heart tugged at his chest with pride. "Indeed she is," he said.

"She's a lovely girl and seems quite sweet, too," Virginia said. Elbowing his arm lightly, she added, "You know, gardeners make the best wives and mothers."

His lips curled up into a grin. "Because . . . ?"

"Because they're patient and nurturing," Virginia explained, "and they know how to coax beauty from even the most barren soil."

Boone nodded. "She's all of those things." He slid his hands into the back pockets of his dungarees. "Would you like to sit down with Belle and talk tomatoes?" Boone was sure Belle would enjoy such a sunny and dynamic woman.

Virginia plucked a pin from her broad-brimmed hat and pulled it off, waving it back and forth like a felt fan to cool her glistening skin. "That sounds wonderful, Boone. Perhaps she and I can eat together sometime at Baker's? That Abigail is a wonderful hostess and a marvelous cook."

"She's the best in town," Boone said, patting his flat stomach. "You go rest up and I'll work on getting you and Belle together for lunch."

Chapter 6

The women would surely have been breaking jailhouse rules had anyone bothered to make any. The "holding cell" set up in Duggan's was currently hosting the Circle Club, whose members were seated both inside and outside the tight space. Amelia had already spent several days and nights in the makeshift jail and was now participating in the club meeting that had come to her.

"I enjoyed the jerky, Sadie," Amelia said, nodding toward her. "Thank Virgil for me, will ya?"

Sadie sat outside the doorway on a stool, as did Hazel, Poppy, and Paulette. She nodded and gave Amelia the okay sign with her thick fingers.

Inside the storage room, Belle sat next to Amelia on the bed, several tins of baked goods set out across the coverlet. Alice had plopped down on the floor cross-legged with her small, wiry-haired dog, Coconut, nestled in her lap.

"And thanks for the visit from Coco yesterday," Amelia said, reaching down to scratch the black mutt's head. "He sure is sweet, but does he always pass so much gas?"

Alice giggled.

"Oh, my," Amelia said, wide-eyed through her thick glasses. "Merle must've thought I'd somehow eaten three cans of baked beans!"

Everyone laughed and Coconut yipped twice, as if in protest.

Because Belle had slept in Duggan's storage room for many years, she knew of a bottom board in the wall that flipped back and forth. Her tabby cat had used it to come and go day and night. A good mouser, Coquina had rid the store of any vermin that had also discovered the swinging panel. When Belle had mentioned the secret door to the women, they couldn't wait to take turns using it to pamper Amelia. While they could have "snuck in" anything by walking straight through the front door, there was something irresistible about this clandestine method. Even Belle had found herself smiling yesterday as she slid a glass jar full of sunflowers through the flap. Over the past two days, Amelia had received a deck of flowery playing cards from Paulette, a Bible dog-eared with personally selected scripture from Poppy, handwritten customer updates from Hazel, huckleberry hand pies from Abigail, and a visit from Alice's gassy pup. Each time Merle saw Amelia devouring a treat or fiddling with whatever gift had just arrived, he'd shake his head while wearing a huge grin across his face.

Belle had deliberately held the meeting after store hours so curious customers wouldn't get a glimpse of the notorious prisoner Polk. News of Amelia's in-store tussle had been splashed across the front page of the *Press*. The headline read:

DON'T POLK THE BEAR!

In the article that followed, Amelia was quoted as saying, "I never shot a gun before, but I guess it's just something that comes natural. You've got to stick up for yourself sometimes."

Belle reached over and put her hand on Amelia's arm. "Would you like to tell us what happened?"

Amelia blew out a long breath and crossed her arms. "As I told Sheriff Clark, I just snapped. After you've been played for a fool by a varmint stealing from you for a week straight, you do what you have to do." She looked down at the little dog. "I may be small, but I know how to take care of myself."

Alice nodded and formed a pistol with her hand. She blew across its pretend muzzle, clearing an imaginary puff of gunpowder.

"We're just so relieved you're all right," Paulette said, and the others nodded in agreement.

"Well, thank you, friends," Amelia said. She leaned to the left so she could see her temporary stand-in. "How's your mother handling your working at my store, Hazel?"

Hazel smoothed her skirt and said, "You mean my working at a 'murderer's store'?" She gazed up at the ceiling and shook her head, her ponytail swishing across her back. "Once again, my mother's behavior is overly dramatic and her statements are uninformed." She looked again at Amelia. "On the other hand, my father has always respected you and has allowed this arrangement . . . temporarily."

"Well, good," Amelia said, and began to plate up hand pies. "Poppy, can Mitchell please just marry Hazel and John Parker so I don't lose my help?"

Hazel offered a soft "Ha!"

Poppy smiled and shrugged. "We'll just have to see how it all unfolds in the Lord's time."

"I say it's our time to eat," Sadie said. She split open her hand pie, gooey purple berries clinging to the golden crust.

Over the next twenty minutes, the conversation covered Paulette's breakfast rendezvous with Duke, the bad batch of oysters at Billy's Saloon, and a wild boar sighting behind the livery stable. Finally, Belle announced that the meeting of the temporarily misshapen Circle Club was over.

"Ladies, thank you from the bottom of my heart for the visit," Amelia said, "and for each and every special treat." To Belle, the tears forming in Amelia's eyes looked huge, magnified by her dense lenses. Not one to show emotion, the druggist joked, "Now, move along. That mean old warden is headed here soon with my stale bread and water."

At that very moment, Merle appeared, carrying a steaming plate of pork ribs alongside mashed potatoes slathered in giblet gravy. "Here's your slop, Polk," Merle said, feigning indifference. Amelia rubbed her palms together while the other ladies exchanged noises of envy and delight. As Coconut whimpered for a taste, Merle shooed the pup and the women out of Duggan's, the jingling of the door's little brass bell nearly muffled by the friends' happy chatter as they said their goodbyes.

Chapter 7

While the rest of the Circle Club was visiting Amelia, Abigail had spent all her free moments poring over a letter to Mr. Edison—rather, three versions of the same letter—trying to convey to him both her credentials and her intentions. Finally, she'd set aside the important project and headed into the kitchen to start dinner. Tinkering, her first love, had long ago been replaced by tending to others. Fortunately, skills that had served her well as an innovator also came in handy as a boardinghouse owner—attention to detail, creative thinking, problem-solving.

"In you go," Abigail said to strips of raw meat, dropping them into a hot skillet.

The aroma of searing beef and sliced garlic began to waft through Baker's. She next added chopped green peppers and onions to the sizzling pan.

"How many mouths tonight?" Boone asked from the top rung of a stepladder across the room. He had his palms pressed up against the kitchen's tin ceiling.

Abigail covered the skillet with a *clang.* "Five, plus one

more I wish I could put a lid on." She bent over and opened the oven door. "The woman *does* have a mouth on her."

Boone let his arms drop to his side. "Loud or annoying?"

"Both," Abigail replied. "She's a birder, and my other guests are so polite that they just let her have the run of the conversation. I think one of my through travelers took an earlier steamer just to escape her descriptions of every single bird on her life list."

"'Life list'?" Boone reached for a rag in his back pocket and began to wipe his hands.

Abigail pushed a tray of lumpy biscuit rounds into the oven. "Apparently, birders keep track of each species they've identified: where they saw it, what it sounded like, what it was eating." Abigail sighed. "Now I'm the one prattling on about birds." She moved to a counter and began snapping the tips off wax beans piled in front of her.

Boone climbed down from the ladder. "Your leak is fixed."

"Hallelujah," Abigail said. "Extra pepper steak for you." She nodded toward the stove. "Speaking of . . . grind some pepper in there, will you?"

Boone fumbled with a myriad of jars filled with spices until he located the pepper mill.

"How are things with you?" Abigail asked while munching on a raw bean.

"Belle seems good," he said, moving toward the stove. "Quiet sometimes, but you know the way she tends to lose herself in the garden until she stops work for the day."

Abigail looked up from the yellow beans. "Whenever I ask you how you are, you tell me how Belle is."

Cranking the handle on the mill, he said, "No I don't." As pepper rained down over the meat, he said, "Tell me when to stop." Abigail instructed him to give two more cranks, which he did. When he was done, he said, "I'm fine." He then replaced the mill and leaned back against the counter. "You?"

Abigail scooped bean tips into a pile and said, "Merle, God love him, has decided he wants to court me properly." She shook her head. "Can you imagine?"

Boone gasped dramatically. "That demon!"

Abigail rolled her eyes. "You know how busy I am." She flung her arm toward the dining room. "My people need constant feeding and watering, and as I mentioned, some of them are a pain in my backside."

Before Abigail could continue, a boarder entered the kitchen, talking.

"Look what I spotted!" the lithe woman exclaimed. She wore a canvas field bag strapped across her narrow body and clutched a slatted wooden basket brimming with ripe carambola. "The Duggan's store man said these look like little bitty stars when you cut them up!" She tilted the basket toward Abigail. "You'll cut up stars for me, won't you, Abi?"

When the woman noticed Boone, her voice turned breathy. "Well, hello there." She set down the basket of yellow fruit and held out a bent palm to him. "I'm Scarlet," she said, preening her long blonde hair with her free hand. "Like the tanager." Keeping her gaze on Boone, she slipped off a pair of binoculars hanging around her neck and held them out toward Abigail. "Be a killdeer and clean off my lenses, won't you, Abi?"

Grabbing a barrel of the binoculars, Abigail widened her eyes and pointed at the woman, mouthing to Boone, "That's her!"

He took Scarlet's outstretched hand. "Boone," he said, his tone flat. He then had to yank away his hand to break loose from her grip.

Abigail circled a dish towel around each lens of the field glasses, watching while Scarlet observed Boone as if he were a coveted bird she'd been waiting to add to her list. She set the binoculars down on the counter with a thud.

"I'm in from Sarasota," the boarder said. "You're probably familiar with my last name . . . Smeltzer?"

Boone shook his head. "Nope."

Scarlet turned her head toward Abigail. "Smeltzer?"

Abigail ignored her and opened the oven door, inhaling the heavenly blend of yeast flirting with butter.

Scarlet sat down at the square wooden dinette and patted the chair next to hers, looking at Boone. He remained at the counter and crossed his arms.

Frowning, Scarlet retied the bird-patterned silk scarf around her neck. "I'm just not having any luck today . . . with anything."

Boone scratched the back of his head below his hat. "Birds not cooperating?"

"Not one bit. They're absolute masters in how *not* to be seen—small, fast, and terribly brownish." She looked at him and perked up, adding in a sensual tone, "But they're also very handsome and useful creatures."

Abigail wound the neck strap around Scarlet's field glasses. "Boone, when is your lovely Belle headed over for lunch with Miss Moore?" She set the binoculars on the table in front of Scarlet and said, "I hope you can see *everything* more clearly now." She locked eyes with the woman and then moved toward the stove to stir the skillet mix.

Scarlet said quickly, "Well, I've got a lovebird, too, and he's quite a find if I do say so myself." Neither Boone nor Abigail inquired further, but she continued. "He was a man-about-town, but now he's just *my* man, *my* husband, and he's as handsome as they come." She rehung the binoculars around her neck.

Abigail swallowed a *pfft* before it could launch from her lips. Several days ago, she'd seen a bulbous, balding man kiss Scarlet goodbye at the wharf and reboard the steamer.

Popping up from her chair, Scarlet announced that she was going to freshen up before dinner. "Nice to meet you, Boone," she said, gripping the leather strap of the binoculars, her fists resting against her chest. "I'm sure you and your mate make a fine"—she paused and looked him up and down—"a very fine pair."

Boone formed bird wings with his hinged hands and flapped them. "Happy hunting."

After Scarlet exited the kitchen, Abigail moved closer to Boone. Quietly, she said, *"Scarlet tanager,* my fanny. That woman is a vulture."

Boone smiled and said, "Now, now . . . *Abi,*" and nudged her with his shoulder.

Chapter 8

A hand-painted sign hanging over the front door of Belle's potting shed read "BB." Boone had explained to her that passersby would assume the letters stood for Baker's Boarding, but that he'd chosen the two letters to represent *Beautiful Belle*. Abigail's several-acre property already had a storage shed, but Boone had wanted Belle to have her own space for gardening supplies and projects. Throughout the weeks-long building process, he kept asking, "What else?" and whatever Belle requested he delivered. After she suggested a weathervane for atop the roof, he found one that featured a crowing rooster with wings flapping. Duke had been happy to part with the piece, his blacksmith shop overrun with metal and brass items he'd collected over the years. Boone had even built the shed on wheels so it could be pulled to wherever he and Belle lived if they married one day.

This afternoon, as Belle waited for Virginia Moore, she studied her special shed, painted a creamy white inside and out, the roof covered with cedar shingles. Moss-green shutters framed its two windows, both anchored by wooden boxes overflowing with orange and yellow lantana, their blossoms irresistible to long-tailed skippers and all pollinators. Boone had even built a small beehouse—an exact replica of the shed—and positioned it on a protected space beneath the roof's overhang. As Belle began to deadhead lantana in one of the flower boxes, she heard a voice behind her.

"You missed one," someone said.

She turned and saw Virginia approaching. The other woman was waving hello.

"Good afternoon, Virginia," Belle said, and dropped the wilted blooms to the ground.

Virginia grinned and gestured toward the flowers. "It's a losing battle trying to keep up with plants, don't you find?"

Belle nodded. "Impossible. Just when I think I've hunted down the very last dead bloom or weed . . ." She smiled.

Virginia surveyed the shed, top to bottom. "She's a real beauty."

"Thank you. Well, thanks to Boone," Belle said. "It's his creation, and I couldn't love it any more than I do." She held her palm out toward the door. "Would you like a look inside?"

"Yes, please." Virginia followed Belle up a small set of portable steps and over the threshold.

Rotating in a slow circle, Virginia whistled as she twirled. "A gardener's dream come true." Next to her was a tall barrel filled with soil. Using the coffee can resting atop the heap, Virginia scooped up a sample and inhaled the aroma. "Oh, my," she gushed.

"I can't take credit," Belle said. "Abigail's compost is as rich as her pound cake."

Virginia smiled. "I imagine your sandy Florida soil needs some heft to help it hold on to nutrients."

The two began to chat about everything inside the shed. An assortment of shovels and rakes hung from pegs along one wall. An old red door with its knob removed lay across two sawhorses and served as a potting table. A ball of gardening twine plugged the empty knob hole. Nearby on the floor, a bait bucket filled with sand housed several tools, their wooden handles sticking up like long, thin stumps.

"I use a quarter cup of mineral oil to one gallon of sand," Belle explained. "The sand cleans the blades and the oil protects against rust."

One corner of the shed was reserved for watering cans of various sizes, two of them with dented spouts. Several wooden crates held stacks of clay pots, castoffs from Baileys' Nursery. Dated gardening magazines were stacked vertically on a shelf, two sturdy flat irons serving as bookends. Clothespins, scissors, and leather journals filled the open drawers of a small periwinkle chest, and on a table stained with water rings sat potted seedlings soaking up the noonday sun.

"That's my cat's favorite spot to nap this time of year," Belle said, pointing to a shelf that hosted warm rays of sunshine.

Virginia tapped her finger on a tackle box next to the napping spot. "I noticed the lures on your hat the other day. Do you fish?"

Belle opened the lid of the red metal box to reveal an array of seed packets. "No," she said, grinning. "It's only for protecting my seeds from hungry mice."

One entire wall of the shed was lined with plants that Belle had selected at Baileys'.

"What's your plan?" Virginia asked, bending over to pinch off a faded flower.

Belle waved her hand over the grouping. "They're for the Edisons' flower boxes. I'm using thrillers, fillers, and spillers." She pointed first to pots of variegated flowers, daisy-shaped with golden rims and orange interiors. "Coreopsis take center stage . . . the thrillers. The pink pentas fill in around them." She bent down and ran a length of bright-green leaves through her hand. "Sweet potato vine will spill out over the sides of the boxes." She looked up at Virginia.

"I think Mina would love that plan," Virginia said. "Hopefully, she and the family can journey south this winter."

"Well, we've found that the Edisons have us prepare as if they will," Belle said, standing up. "Ever optimistic."

Just then, the deep *bong-bong* of a ship's bell rang out across the yard from Baker's, signaling a meal was ready.

"How about some lunch?" Belle asked.

"Another very good plan," Virginia said, and followed Belle out of the pretty little shed.

• • •

Abigail had set the kitchen dinette for Belle and Virginia so they could enjoy lunch away from the buzz of boarders eating in the dining room. She was scurrying between both places, transporting plates and pitchers as they entered.

"Have a seat, ladies," Abigail instructed over her shoulder. "I'll dish you up."

Once Belle and Virginia were settled in, their plates heaped with braised venison and steaming mustard greens, Virginia asked, "So, have you any experience with canning, Belle?"

Belle poked at the greens with her fork to cool them down. "I've helped Abigail over the years, mostly with her bread-and-butter pickles. String beans and carrots, too."

"I see," Virginia said, smoothing the napkin in her lap. "As Boone mentioned to you, tomatoes are the focus of my program. They're relatively easy to grow and, I'd imagine, especially so here, what with your forgiving climate and well-draining soil."

Belle scooted a turtle-shaped saltcellar closer to Virginia. "Boone told me you've determined that canning tomatoes is a way for rural girls to learn outside the classroom."

"Yes, to learn *and* earn," Virginia said. "Gardens and kitchens are wonderful classrooms, and when girls become knowledgeable about canning and selling their products, tomatoes equal money." She buttered a thick slice of rye bread.

Virginia went on to explain that U.S. agricultural agencies had recently organized corn clubs to teach boys—instead of their sometimes-reticent parents—updated farming techniques. Contests were held where young men competed for highest crop yields, which earned them money and demonstrated more efficient farming methods to the boys' families and their neighbors. When Marie Cromer, a schoolteacher in the small town of Aiken, South Carolina, heard about corn clubs, she and other educators asked why girls weren't getting in on the fun and financial gains. Soon after, the U.S. Department of Agriculture responded, selecting tomatoes for the girls' crop. A group of former educators—including Virginia—then began pioneering the tomato club movement across several southern states. Whereas boys farmed their corn crops on one-acre plots, girls' tomato patches covered just one-tenth of an acre, a more manageable size for young ladies between the ages of nine and eighteen. Club members worked in groups to can the produce, and then each girl marketed their wares in the local community. Virginia explained that for the first time, these "tomato girls" had money to put toward schoolbooks and even college. Prizes were being awarded at county and state fairs, too—everything from cash to calves and chickens.

"I was working for Tennessee's Department of Education to improve conditions in our rural schools when I was asked to also begin organizing canning clubs for country girls," Virginia explained. Home demonstration agents like her were advised to visit schools, discuss tomato clubs, and leave enrollment forms with teachers. "Young women everywhere have longings and aspirations that tomato clubs can help them realize right at home. Yes, jobs in the Northeast are drawing people cityward, but some have described that migration as the funeral procession of our rural nation." She laid down her fork and wiped table crumbs onto her napkin. "Does any of this sound interesting to you?"

Raising her eyebrows, Belle asked, "Are you suggesting I try your idea here?"

Several boarders entered the kitchen, dropped off empty teacups, and headed for the screen door.

"Yes, Belle. I'm wondering if you might like to take a small step toward creating a tomato club in Fort Myers."

At the mention of her name, Belle noticed a woman in the small group turn her head and stare at her. She wore a silk scarf decorated with colorful birds tied under her chin. *The rude bandit,* Belle thought, remembering the woman she'd encountered heading toward the estate.

The boarder fiddled with the scarf and stuck the tip of her tongue out at Belle. Then she left, the screen door slamming shut behind her and the others.

Appalled but unruffled, Belle returned her gaze to Virginia. "I like any idea that encourages women . . . or girls. The members of our women's club certainly try to support one another."

Virginia leaned in, her eyes twinkling. "What if you worked with just two girls in town and taught them to grow and can tomatoes? If they do well, they might qualify for Florida's state competition in a few months."

Belle reached for a pitcher of tea that Abigail had placed on the table. "Um, that may not be the best idea, Virginia." She topped off their glasses. "I'm quite good with plants, but beyond that . . ."

"For heaven's sake, you've already organized a women's club, Belle," Virginia said, "and from the sound of it, it's a success." She added softly, "Right?"

Belle shrugged. "I suppose so, but you're a teacher, Virginia. You have experience working with young people."

With a grin, Virginia said, "You were a young girl once . . ."

Belle sipped tea and stayed quiet for a minute. "I'd hate to fail a little girl."

Tilting her head, Virginia said, "I'm surprised a gardener would say such a thing." She folded her hands in her lap. "Gardeners are optimists, firm believers that the time and care they invest will one day make the world a more beautiful place for everyone. And if nature decides otherwise, we gardeners roll up our sleeves and dig in the dirt again . . . until we succeed."

Belle sat up a little straighter. "I suppose that's true." She gently swung the long braid of hair resting on her chest around to her back. "Why don't you tell me more about the clubs?"

Pushing away her empty plate, Virginia began to share details about the program. She explained that men were allowed to plow the one-tenth acre, but the young women were then responsible for everything else related to growing, harvesting, and canning their tomatoes.

"Each girl must create what's called a tomato club booklet, which includes her reasons for joining the club plus details about her project, like insect control and watering schedules," Virginia said. "The girls even illustrate their booklet covers and bind them with a decorative ribbon."

Belle nodded, imagining one of Hazel's red silk ribbons tied through a booklet. She considered pitching the idea as a Circle Club project, which made accepting the challenge seem less intimidating.

Virginia explained that during in-person competitions, prizes were awarded for largest yield, best displays, largest and most perfect tomato, and finest collection of tomato recipes. Even if their crops failed, girls were allowed to compete without tomatoes, club songs and booklets also being factors in the participants' overall scores.

"You've got the gardening part down, Belle, and surely Abigail would be willing to refresh your canning skills. I'll provide plenty of information, too." She leaned on the table with crossed arms. "I don't know you well, but I've got a pretty good eye for potential." She smiled. "I'll bet you'd do quite well alongside a pair of local girls."

Before Belle could react, Abigail approached the table carrying two slices of pie, cinnamon-flecked apples spilling out onto the plates. "Dessert?" she asked, setting down the treats before either woman could answer.

"Abigail, I must commend you," Virginia said, eyeing the flaky triangle. "You are every bit the stellar hostess Mina said you'd be. Thank you."

"Well, I love what I do, and—" Abigail was interrupted by the sound of something shattering on the dining room floor. She chuckled. "Most days. Please excuse me."

Virginia smiled and then cut into her pie. "You'll at least think about it, Belle?"

Belle spun her plate so her slice, like the tip of an arrow, pointed directly at her. "I certainly will."

Chapter 9

When Belle entered Duggan's, she heard the familiar cadence of coins dropping into the till of a cash register, a cozy reminder of the many years she'd spent there.

As a teenager, she'd been fascinated by the wide range of wares in the general store—decorative crocks, towers of spices, and glass cases filled with razors, hair combs, hat pins, and fans. Hooped barrels held pickles and crackers, their lids obliging an occasional game of checkers. Her work tasks had ranged from dusting the cut-crystal cruet sets to stacking bars of soap and folding jersey overshirts. She was always on the lookout for new merchandise, and never missed a chance to examine Merle's prized rattlesnake rattle displayed on the front counter in an ornate porcelain ashtray.

Merle had also served as the town's postmaster during many of the years she lived with him, and in that time he often let her perform the "fancy cancels" on envelopes. She'd grip a cork that had been carved into his signature diamond shape and touch it to an ink pad. Then she'd cancel each stamp to ensure no one else could use it.

Over the years, interacting with customers became more

natural for her, and after a while she genuinely enjoyed keeping up with people's lives. When the last shopper left and the "Closed" sign hung in the window, Belle would tidy up shelves as Merle counted the day's earnings, the two of them swapping updates on how neighbors were faring—whose hip was hurting or who could use the Helpful Hamper, a basket packed with staples left on the doorstep of a down-on-their-luck family. She truly missed working alongside Merle, but it was he—and Abigail—who'd helped launch her from Duggan's, while still lending the support she needed to be able to explore a life beyond the comfortable but sheltered existence she'd lived there.

"Belley!" Merle greeted her as she strolled in and relocked the door behind her. She'd used a key hidden under a pot of basil to let herself in. He walked out from behind the counter to give her a hug.

"Hi, Merle," she said into his broad chest. When they separated, she asked, "How was the day?"

Pulling out two stools, he replied, "Well, we had a run on watermelons." Patting the one remaining melon, he reassured it, "You'll sell tomorrow." He nodded toward a stool. "Have a seat."

Belle sat and breathed in familiar scents—smoky breakfast bacon, briny pickle water. After the pair had spent a few minutes catching up on the rest of the doings at Duggan's, Belle asked, "Have you met Mina's friend Virginia Moore yet?"

Merle reached beside the cash register for a glass of whiskey, an evening staple, along with the nightly Cuban cigar he hadn't yet lit. "Yes, she stopped in earlier. Nice gal. She gushed about Abigail, which of course makes me like her even more." He took a sip. "That's more than I can say for some flighty little thing who came in the other day. She was bragging about birds and grumbling about the food at Baker's to several of my customers."

"What?!" Belle said, lightly slapping the counter.

"Don't you worry. As I rang up her carambola, I asked when her steamer home was scheduled." He poked his thumb toward a bushel of onions. "I'll pop a little goodbye present in her luggage." He rubbed his palms together. "Got a few in there about to go bad."

Belle shook her finger. "Merle . . ." But then she put her hand to one side of her mouth. "A head of garlic wouldn't hurt either."

Merle chuckled and eased himself off the stool. "What can I fix you to drink? The usual?" He disappeared behind the counter and began to rattle glassware.

"Please," she said, and twirled in her seat to face him. "Today I had lunch with Virginia, and I agree . . . she's quite nice."

As he squeezed a bit of juice from an orange into a glass of water for her, Merle shook his head. "Boone said Norville behaved like some sort of jolly joker during her visit . . . as if he'd jumped out of a deck of cards and landed right in front of her."

Belle raised her eyebrows. "Really?" She lightly fluffed a vase full of bee balm blooms on the counter. "Well, she does have a way of making a person feel . . . special."

Merle set the glass in front of Belle. "You are special, honey."

She drew in a breath and sighed lightly. "I don't know . . ."

Merle squinted at Belle. "What is it? You can tell me."

And she could. Candid conversations between the pair now flowed easily, as they had ever since they'd navigated their way through an alarming revelation last year. Right there in Duggan's, Belle had confronted Merle about a significant detail of their relationship that he'd failed to tell her. The secret had been accidentally revealed to Belle by Poppy, who'd assumed the two had already discussed the matter.

Through tears, Merle had admitted to Belle that he and his

then soon-to-be-wife, Clara, had intended to adopt her after her mother died, but then Clara died suddenly from a rattlesnake bite. Without Clara, he'd been ill-equipped to care for a newborn, and Mr. Carson, whose baby had drowned, had told Poppy and Pastor Peck that he and his wife were open to adoption. The Pecks prayed with Merle as he mourned Clara and worked through the decision to let Belle go.

When she'd confronted Merle about this jarring omission—they'd lived together for more than a decade at that point—he'd admitted it was true, weeping and apologizing for the pain she'd suffered at the hands of her adoptive brother. As angry and shocked as she was in that moment, Belle had quickly decided to spare Merle the ugly truth about her life under the same roof with an abusive deviant. She let Merle believe that the only thing Julius used his greedy, grubby hands for was to slap her, to bloody her cheek and bruise her eye the night she ran to Duggan's. Since that fateful day, Merle and Abigail had raised and loved her. How could she possibly feel anything but gratitude? And so, she'd forgiven Merle and assured him that he'd merely done what he thought was best for her as a child. That difficult conversation had further strengthened their devotion to one another, and now the pair could talk openly about nearly anything.

"Virginia wants me to try something called a tomato club here in town," Belle said. "I'd need to choose two girls and teach them how to grow and can tomatoes."

Merle hooked both thumbs around his suspenders. "Huh. A club of two?"

Belle nodded. "It would be an experiment of sorts, and I'd like the Circle Club to help."

"Well, you wouldn't be the first to experiment around here," Merle quipped.

She grinned at the reference to her employer. "Gardening

I know how to do. But guiding young people . . ." Belle paused and tapped a finger on the counter for a moment. "At the funeral, Etta Dunn called Betsy a sad excuse for a mother."

Merle snapped his suspenders. "That dang Etta. Her arms are going to fall off from stirring the pot so often. The woman just can't seem to help herself. And at a funeral, no less."

Belle folded her hands in her lap. "Was I considered a sad excuse for a little girl when I lived with the Carsons?"

"Honey . . ." Merle eased around the counter and sat across from Belle. "Let's untangle this a bit."

• • •

For a second, Merle saw Belle once again as a shy little girl in his store, eyeing the raspberry samples. As he always had, he just wanted to comfort her.

"Merle, be honest. When I still lived with them, did people talk about me? See me as troubled?" Belle asked.

"Of course not," he said. "The Carsons kept to themselves except for Sunday church and sugarcane grinds. How could anyone possibly know what kind of mother Betsy was?"

Not now, not ever would Merle share with Belle the whispers he'd overheard in Duggan's after he took her in. *Are we just giving away children in our town now?* or *She lives in Merle's storage room!* He was quite sure he hadn't heard the bulk of it; gossip was always traded behind the back of its target. Indeed, the circumstances behind Belle's extraction from the Carson family had been unclear—even to him. But all that mattered was that Belle had run to him, bleeding and bruised, and that when he'd informed Nelson Carson that Belle would now live with him, no one in the family had fought to keep her. From that day on, he and Abigail had focused only on loving and raising Belle.

Merle reached over and patted her hands. "You were a

fine young girl. Curious, kind, and always a welcomed sight at Duggan's."

She shrugged and traced the rim of her glass with a fingertip.

"You'll be a wonderful teacher to young girls, Belle. I just know it," Merle said.

The pair sat quietly for a moment. Merle wished Abigail were sitting beside him. Through the years, she always knew what to say whenever Belle needed a boost. Abigail just made soothing souls look easy. *Oh, c'mon, Merle,* he said to himself. He shifted on the stool and gave it a shot in her absence.

"Honey, when we push through hardships—and you have—we get stronger." He gestured toward a shelf on the wall holding glass canisters filled with loose tea. "Think about those tea leaves. They get packed into a strainer and then dunked into boiling hot water—over and over. But the result is good, strong tea, right?"

Belle nodded but then started to giggle. She covered her mouth with her hand and mumbled, "I'm sorry, Merle."

His serious face immediately became animated. He slapped the counter and started to laugh. "Oh hell. I'm no Abigail, am I?"

Belle shook her head and laughed again. "I appreciate you trying to support me, though."

Merle admitted, "Those dang tea canisters were right in my line of sight . . ."

They joked and chatted for a bit and then Merle scooted off his stool.

Taking Belle's hand in his, he said, "Let's go pick out a smelly onion for that uppity boarder, honey."

Chapter 10

"I'm so pleased Belle has agreed to give the tomato club a whirl," Virginia said, cradling her plump purse as if it were a baby.

Abigail had once again jammed it full of goodies, this time for Virginia's steamer ride home following her short stay. She, Virginia, and Merle were standing outside Baker's, surrounded by luggage that had been set out by boarders. Virginia and Belle had already said their goodbyes before Belle went to work next door.

"She'll have a lot of help from the Circle Club members. Each of the women has unique gifts, as we all do," Abigail told Virginia.

"And these are two of mine," Merle joked, flexing his biceps. "Now, which one is your bag? I'll take it down to the wharf."

"That's kind of you, Merle. It's the Gladstone with my monogram printed on the front," Virginia said.

When Merle located the bag, he ran a fingertip across three gold letters presented in the traditional order of a monogram: the first initial, last initial (printed larger), and middle initial. "'V.M.P.' I know the *V* and the *M* . . ." He raised his eyebrows at Virginia.

"Pearl," she said, and smiled.

"All right, let's get V.M.P. to her steamer," Abigail directed. "Merle, thank you, and would you also take this one down?" She winked at him, knowing he had a special parting gift to sneak into the Smeltzer woman's bag. Merle had told Abigail about the birder disparaging her food; plus, she didn't like the way Scarlet had flirted with Boone. While Baker's reputation was of the utmost importance to her, Abigail wasn't concerned that their smelly scheme would tarnish it. Surely this annoying woman complained about everything and garnered little respect from the caliber of boarder Abigail hoped to attract. *Plant that onion,* she thought.

As Merle headed for the wharf, Abigail moved closer to Virginia.

The other departing boarders were still milling around inside the house, but she lowered her voice anyway.

"Virginia, I wonder if you'd deliver something to Mrs. Edison for me." Abigail had met Mina last year when she was in town to hire a gardener for the estate. "This information is actually for Mr. Edison." She held out a large packet.

Virginia didn't hesitate. "Of course I'll help." She grinned. "I can't fit it into my bag . . . but that's your fault."

The women laughed, and Abigail tucked the envelope between Virginia's arm and her bulging purse. No questions or answers were exchanged. She'd sensed that would be the case and greatly appreciated Virginia's discretion. Abigail's intention was simply to help.

And the fewer people who knew about her daring gesture, the better.

Chapter 11

Scarlet's husband was out of town, doing whatever it was he did to provide them with a lavish lifestyle, including the stately home she'd just entered, its paintings and fabrics dominated by bird themes. The mister, she recalled, had taken a schooner from Sarasota to Tampa Bay for something involving sponges. Or maybe oranges? The words sounded similar, and as much as she tried to act interested in his business doings, she knew that *her* job was simply to be the most attractive version of herself. One and one made two, and in their marriage, she was the one tasked with adding *pretty* to the equation. Unfortunately, her hubby was a master of both subtraction and addition—thinning hair and a substantial waistline that kept on growing. At least their bank account was following the same trajectory as his weight.

"Donald!" she yelled. "Bag, please!" She was in her bedroom after returning from her trip to Fort Myers. She'd found the town and its residents—barring one—as lackluster as a female cowbird. Reaching down into her purse, she removed a pair of binoculars and set them on her dresser.

As she did, a tall man knocked on her open door and

entered the room. He was holding her luggage at arm's length, and his eyes were pinched nearly shut.

"Here you go, Mrs. Smeltzer." He set down the bag and quickly left the room, closing the door behind him.

Scarlet frowned. Donald was always brief in his interactions, but his odd expression and swift exit was curious. Then abruptly, something changed in the room. She sniffed and then sniffed again.

"What is *that*?!" she said, fanning the air with both hands.

At no point in her trip had she handled her bag—she rarely did—so this was her first close encounter with it. She stared at her luggage on the floor in front of her. Was *it* the source of the putrid odor suddenly defiling her perfectly appointed bedroom? She knelt in front of the bag and held her breath as she struggled to unbuckle both straps. Starved for oxygen, she sucked in air through her clenched teeth. When she finally released the straps and opened the bag, both compartments hit the floor. Instantly, an invisible attacker assaulted her nostrils.

"Ew!" Scarlet squealed. She fell back onto her bottom and frantically tried to wave away the stink.

With the bag's contents fully exposed, the rancid odor was allowed to stretch its vile wings and soar around the room.

"This is outrageous!" she yelled. Confused and furious, she began to dig through the dresses and undergarments in the bag. Before long, her hand collided with the slimy culprit—a rotten onion.

"Donald!" she screamed. Who would *dare* treat a Smeltzer this way?

Fuming, she began to recall every person she'd met in that insipid, no-good town called Fort Myers.

Chapter 12

The first day of September greeted Fort Myers with a wet wallop. In the late afternoon, black clouds snuck up on a clear blue sky, thunder growling as the storm advanced. When Belle saw lightning needles prick the horizon, she moved the women's meeting from Krayer's Guava Grove to the Methodist church, yet one more venue she'd managed to procure on short notice. Even after a year of club meetings, Belle could never seem to secure a permanent space, requiring her to drop off postcards with meeting details at each member's residence. If she ever had a home large enough one day, she'd be delighted to host every gathering of the Circle Club.

Now, torrents of rain slapped at the windows of the old church, lit up with candles to counter the storm's pall. Paulette was playing a spirited hymn on the piano to further brighten the mood, and the ladies were chatting. Abigail's refreshments were set out on the makeshift altar, a wooden table that on Sundays was draped with a long white cloth. Today it was covered with lemon bars, braided cheese straws, and pear wedges. Amelia took charge of passing out plates filled with snacks.

"Everyone ready?" Belle said, accepting a plate.

Signaling an end to the pre-meeting chat, Paulette performed a dazzling glissando across the piano keys. Alice added a loud "Ta-da!" making the other women laugh.

Once they'd each claimed a space in a pew and faced each other as comfortably as possible, Belle spoke.

"Welcome back, Amelia," she said, and the other women acknowledged her return.

"Thank you, ladies," Amelia said. "Hazel, you did a fine job at Polk's in my absence, and I'm so pleased you're staying on with me for a while."

Hazel nodded toward Amelia as the other women expressed their congratulations.

Shuffling through her notes, Belle said, "I've got some news to announce."

Just then, an intensely bright flash was followed instantly by a clap of thunder, rattling every candlestick in the room.

The women jumped in their seats and several screeched. They sat in silence for a few seconds.

"Lordy," Sadie said, and knocked her knuckles on the pew's cap rail. "Hope that bolt didn't mess with our patched-up bell."

"Sounded more like our bird-of-paradise may no longer be with us," Amelia suggested, and the women spent a few more moments speculating about the proximity of the close lightning strike.

Once they'd settled down, Belle continued. "As you all may know, Mina's friend Virginia Moore was in town last week."

Alice interjected. "Long coat, fast walk, gave Coconut a good pet on Duggan's porch. I like her."

Belle smiled. "That's Virginia, all right. She's involved with a program in several southern states that helps rural girls become more confident, have fun, and make some money." Belle held up a seed packet featuring a ripe red tomato. "And these are the key." She rotated the packet in a half circle so each woman could see it. "Who knew a tomato could change lives?"

"I sure didn't," Poppy said, and took a small bite of her cheese straw. "How does it work?"

"I'm still reading through the pamphlets Virginia gave me," Belle said, "but learning by doing is the basic idea. Girls plant, grow, and can tomatoes while learning skills like math and economics as they work."

"Why tomatoes?" Alice asked, stroking Coconut, the mutt still shaking from the sudden boom.

"Good question, Alice." Belle flipped through her notes. "Tomatoes are apparently high in acidity, which means they can be safely preserved using just boiled water, not the high-pressure cooking equipment rural people don't have. Plus, tomatoes are a relatively easy crop to grow and process." Belle looked up from her notes. "Basically, tomatoes help young girls learn and earn."

Hazel smiled and tightened the bow around her thick ponytail. "Oh, this is good. My mother will be apoplectic when she hears about this."

Sadie chuckled. "Guess we'll add 'maters to the list of things that irk your mama, Hazel."

Belle had no doubt that Ida would be both irked by and opposed to efforts to cultivate independent young women. Hazel had told the group that her mother talked incessantly about the importance of *domesticity* and constantly reminded her that *a lady should always put herself second to the needs of her husband, children, and proper maintenance of the home.*

Belle despised the way Ida considered herself, and the Cravin name, elite and beyond reproach. Yet her perfume was stale and her attitude sour. Belle had even accidentally caught a glimpse of Ida dallying with a cow hunter in a storage closet at the Palms Hotel last year.

She'd been standing on a ladder trimming a Calusa grape vine the moment her eyes were poisoned. Though she tried her best to never judge others, the shocking sight had been a revolting confirmation of the married woman's hypocrisy.

Clearly, Ida's word meant nothing, and her sharp tongue was as distasteful as her secret behavior. She frequently offended her own customers at Cravin's, where she oversaw the local circulation of mail.

Well, Myra, it appears you haven't received a letter from your son in quite a spell, Ida might say, followed by a *tsk-tsk.* Or, while pinching her nose she might advise, *Our soap and razors are in the back, Clem.*

To Belle, the sallow-faced woman was not only mean but a fraud, too. Always dressed as if heading for Sunday service, she worshipped only prestige and control. It was no surprise to Belle that the Bible Ida carried was in pristine condition. By comparison, Poppy's book was dog-eared and bent on all corners from her relentless quest to serve the Lord.

Clearing her throat, Belle shooed Ida from her thoughts and continued explaining tomato clubs to the group. "Virginia suggested I work with two girls to start, and immediately I knew I wanted all of you to help me." She rattled the seed packet. "This seems like a worthy project for us, doesn't it?"

"So, the Circle Club would support the Tomato Club?" Paulette asked.

"That's the plan," Belle confirmed, "and Virginia will register us with the Florida chapter of home demonstration. We'll represent Lee County, and if our group qualifies, we'll compete in the state competition in Sarasota."

The ladies exchanged smiles, and Alice rubbed her hands together before she spoke. "What should we call the club?"

Belle looked up from a pamphlet. "You did a good job naming our club, Alice, but I'm afraid your creativity won't be needed this time. The clubs are named after the counties they represent."

"So, we would be the Lee County Girls' Tomato Club," Hazel deduced.

"Ick, boring," Alice noted.

Belle smiled. "I agree, but there will be plenty of opportunity for each of us to be creative in the ways we help the girls."

"Speaking of," Sadie said. "Any ideas about which girls to choose?" She took a significant bite of a lemon bar and waited for suggestions.

"It seems obvious to me," Paulette said. She looked around the group. "Fae and Mazie Dawson."

Poppy made the sign of the cross and softly said, "Rest in peace."

Last year, the sisters' parents had died from pulmonary tuberculosis, just a week apart. The devastated ten- and twelve-year-old had since moved in with their uncle Clay and his sister, Edwina. Clay worked long hours at his cabinet shop, and Edwina, nearly forty, did her best to keep up with the demands of raising two young girls. Neighbors pitched in as often as they could but were busy rearing their own families.

"I like that idea," Amelia said as she looked around the group. "Staying within one family helps us keep from hurting other girls' feelings."

Belle liked the idea, too, having often thought about the Dawson girls after their parents died. She understood their pain, being a fellow orphan, but their history was quite different from hers. Having lost her mother upon entering the world, Belle had always longed to know what Eva was like; the Dawson girls had known their loving mama and ached to have her back. The sisters had also lost their father—doubly tragic—while Belle had never had a father to lose. Before the Dawson parents' deaths, Belle had chatted casually with the couple—and with their cute little daughters—whenever they'd crossed paths. But, since the tragedy, she hadn't seen much of the girls. Clay and Edwina had been keeping their nieces close, most likely bonding with them as best they could while navigating their rough new journey. Belle rode to their house now and then, but only to weed the gardens.

"Surely everyone will rally around our decision to help support the girls," Poppy said.

"Not everybody," Hazel said, her smile sly.

"All right, then," Belle said. "Show of hands for all those who'd like me to approach the Dawsons."

Every hand went up; Hazel used both.

"Well, there you have it, Belle," Sadie said, shifting in the pew. "Get ready to start talkin' tomatoes."

Belle nodded. "Talking, and then—I hope—digging." Gathering up her notes, she recalled the girls' sweet faces and Virginia's inspiring words.

Gardeners are firm believers that the time and care they invest will one day make the world a more beautiful place for everyone.

Chapter 13

Dawson's Cabinets was just down the road from Duggan's, so Merle often walked along Front Street to visit its owner, Clay, a fellow businessman and fine conversationalist. This morning, Merle was dodging numerous puddles as he headed over half an hour before his own store opened. He knew hardworking Clay would already be in his shop, building something that would be useful to his fellow townsfolk, now or as they crossed into the next life.

As he approached Dawson's, Merle walked by a plate-sized whirligig that sat atop a wooden post near the shop's entrance. Clay had built it several years ago, perhaps wanting to create something whimsical for a change. It featured four miniature sloops that spun in a circle whenever the breeze filled their cloth sails. The little boats were painted red and amused many a child on days they "set sail." Today, though, the motionless boats were caught in the doldrums. After several days of intense storms, the air was finally still.

"Mornin', Clay," Merle said, and handed his friend a mug of steaming coffee inside the shop. "Figured you're drinking that brown gargle you make, so I brought the good stuff. Brewed the Duggan's way."

Clay smiled, put down his hammer, and took the mug. "The way-too-strong way, but I'll accept it."

The men clinked their mugs together.

"Still working on the Ardmore casket?" Merle asked. He took his regular seat, a rocker that featured a striped cushion sewn and stuffed by Edwina.

"Yes, and I'm dying to finish it," Clay said with a wink.

The men could engage in gallows humor because Ben Ardmore had lived a long and fruitful life. That hadn't been the case for Clay's relatives—at least the *long* part. Merle couldn't imagine the torture Clay had endured last year, building coffins for his younger brother and sister-in-law. Since their fatal illnesses, Merle had dropped in more often on Clay, a good man overwhelmed by the bad draw that had befallen people he loved dearly. Merle figured perhaps he could offer Clay an ear or some small nuggets of wisdom, having himself raised a fourteen-year-old girl. Or maybe he could just bring him a quality cup of coffee.

"I hear Belle stopped in to see you and the girls," Merle said, pushing off with his boots to set the chair in motion.

Clay had already swapped his coffee mug for a wood plane. Gripping both handles, he ran the tool across one side of the casket, using firm, decisive strokes. "Yep. She came by the house last night. The girls really like her." Curled shavings dropped to the floor from the back of the plane. "Edwina and I agree that a project would be good for the girls."

"Well, glad to hear it, Clay." Merle was very pleased by the family's decision and hadn't had a chance yet to learn of it from Belle.

Just then, Edwina came through the shop door, carrying a plate with a cloth napkin draped over it. She and Clay were in their late thirties, but Edwina looked much older, her hair already fully grayed. Because neither had married, the siblings lived together, an arrangement that made caring for the girls less complicated.

"Good morning, men," Edwina said. "Here's your breakfast, Clay." She set the plate down on his workbench along with silverware. "Didn't know you'd be here, Merle, or I'd have scrambled more eggs."

Merle slowly shook his head. "Well, well. King Clay. Gets his breakfast made . . . his coffee brought to him. I'm surprised you haven't built yourself a throne yet."

Edwina laughed. "Give it to him, Merle."

Clay grinned and pretended to adjust his invisible crown.

"So, how are the girls, Edwina?" Merle got up and pulled over a chair for her.

"Thanks, Merle, but I can't linger." She crossed her arms. "Depends on the day with those two. Sad on Monday, angry on Tuesday, fine on Wednesday. They fight a lot, but that could just be their ages. Lord knows we're all still in a bit of shock."

Clay stopped working and set down the plane on the floor of the casket. "Edwina is exhausted, and neither of us has any idea how to raise kids, Merle. The only thing I know how to do well," he said, patting the box, "is knocking together six sides." He shrugged. "These young girls? A mystery."

"Well, Clay, all females are a mystery," Merle said. He turned toward Edwina and sat back down. "No offense intended. I just mean that men and women are different for a reason. If Abigail wasn't there to help me raise Belle, I would have been lost. So many times, she knew what to do or say when I didn't." He recalled his recent tea mishap with Belle. "Still don't."

"Oh, I'm sure you did the same for Abigail, Merle," Edwina said, tucking a thin gray strand behind her ear.

Clay chewed on his lip. "We're a year in now, and the girls

eat and sleep well. They do their schoolwork. Maybe the bickering is because they're still trying to feel at home."

"Could be," Merle said. "For me, silence was worse when it came to Belle. At least when your girls are bickering, they're talking." He lightly tapped the rocker's arms with his thumbs. "Sounds to me like you two are doing a fine job with them. You're both doing your best."

"Well, you and Abigail certainly raised a lovely woman, Merle," Edwina said. "To be honest, Clay and I may not have agreed to this tomato project had someone else asked."

Merle smiled. "I'm sure glad you did. I'll bet Belle learns as much from your girls as they do from her."

Edwina sighed. "Tomatoes, rutabagas, cantaloupes. Whatever helps those girls, I'm for." She turned toward the door. "I'll be back to pick up your dishes later, Clay. So long, Merle."

After Edwina left, Merle decided to keep the conversation light. "Got a project for you if you're willing, Clay. I'll pay you to build a special gift for Abigail."

Clay raised his eyebrows. "A gift for Abigail? I can't build a one-way train ticket to get rid of ya."

"Oh, so you're a funny king, are you?" Merle said.

The men teased each other a bit more, then Merle proceeded to explain to Clay what he needed for his gal, so he could—finally—court her properly.

Chapter 14

Boone was headed for Polk's when he happened upon a sullen Norville Decker standing outside the caretaker's cottage. His untucked shirttails were flapping in the breeze.

"I'm lonely and I'm lovesick," Decker said, his normally animated hands at rest, his bony shoulders hunched.

Immediately Boone responded. "No. Uh-uh." He waved his finger back and forth between them. "We aren't . . . we don't . . . nope."

"But I miss my Tennessee treasure," Decker whined, and hung his head. Several weeks had passed since Virginia had departed. "She and I . . ."

Boone interrupted. "C'mon, Decker. You barely know Virginia."

The caretaker sniffled and twisted his pouty face up toward Boone. "So what?"

Boone held up one finger after another with each word. "You. Just. Met. Her. Decker." Yes, he and Belle had fallen in love quickly, but they'd shared so much—losses, secrets, dreams. Decker and Virginia had only shared one stroll around the property. Ridiculous.

The dejected man's face changed from looking sad to appearing annoyed. "Do you remember when you had your first piece of pecan pie?"

"Stop, Decker." Boone started to walk away, shaking his head. "We don't talk about pie. We don't talk about women . . ." Sometimes he just couldn't abide Decker's quirks, and this mopey-dopey routine was a new and particularly annoying one.

Decker yelled in Boone's direction. "You fell in love with that slice of pie of yours on the very first bite, didn't you? The first bite!"

Boone kept walking and even began to jog slightly to get away more quickly. He had more important things to do than indulge Decker's half-baked heartbreak.

• • •

Standing in what was to be the Dawson girls' new tomato field, Belle caught the thick scent of manure on the breeze. Amelia's apothecary was located right next to the town's livery, so customers often got a whiff of horses, hay, and the by-product of that combination. Amelia had told the club she'd known that pungent odors were a risk when she'd purchased the property, but she'd bought it anyway because the parcel was expansive. Her hope, she'd explained, was to someday build an additional structure for a quilt shop called Polk's Pick Stitch. But, right now, on this September afternoon, Amelia's extra acreage had worked out nicely for a one-tenth-acre tomato field.

"Girls," Belle said, "make sure to turn the soil." Using a pitchfork, she was teaching Fae and Mazie how to work compost and manure into the rows Boone was creating using a disc harrow. He was seated atop the harrow, maneuvering the pair of horses pulling the plow, its two gangs of concave metal discs shooting soil in opposite directions.

Belle had invited Alice to join her and the girls in the field, while the other women gathered at a picnic table behind Polk's, where Amelia was inside working. She'd noticed that Alice was gifted at managing the somewhat-moody sisters, perhaps because she was closest to them in age. Just last week, the girls had begun arguing as the women were showing them drawings of pesky tomato hornworms in a gardening magazine. Alice diffused the squabble by simply asking the girls, "What's wrong?" Turned out they'd simply been hungry and in need of a snack.

"This stuff smells awful," Fae whined as she poked at the soil. Mazie joined in. "Our tomatoes are going to taste like horse plop."

Alice didn't skip a beat. "Now, that's the spirit, ladies." She crossed her arms and her eyes.

Both girls laughed and began to work their pitchforks with a bit more vigor.

Bless you, Alice, Belle thought. She was a bit concerned about whether the sisters could endure the long haul required to grow tomatoes. Not to mention canning them. How thankful she was to have the support of her Circle Club friends!

"Looks like the booklet should be tied with a red or green ribbon," Hazel said, reading from literature spread out on the picnic table. "I've got both colors."

Paulette lightly cleared her throat. "Since I'm in charge of helping with the song, I'm going to encourage the girls to come up with a few words they consider important . . . like *seeds* and *growth*." She wrote down a few words of her own.

"We know that Paul says, 'For whatsoever a man soweth, that shall he also reap,'" Poppy said, smiling. "Every one of us is a farmer, scattering spiritual seeds across the field of life. Seeds of grace, joy, love, anger, and hatred." She drummed her fingers on her Bible and looked around the table. "That's not helpful, is it?"

The other women laughed and Poppy did, too. When they spotted Fae and Mazie in the field pretending to ride their pitchforks like stick horses—and Alice yelling "Yee haw!"—they laughed even harder.

. . .

The women's backs were facing Polk's, so at first no one noticed Ida Cravin surveying the scene. When they finally took note, Ida turned and walked rapidly into the store.

"What's your little club up to, Amelia?" she snapped at the store owner, who was standing behind the counter.

Amelia stifled a yawn with the back of her hand. "Here to pick up your liver pills, Ida?"

"Yes," she said, and yanked open her purse to search for payment. "You should know that my followers and I *do not* approve of whatever's going on out there."

Amelia leaned to the left, looking behind Ida. "I don't see any followers, Ida. Seems to me you're not a leader . . . you're just out for a walk by yourself."

Ida stamped her foot. "If you know what's good for you and this town, you'll put a stop to whatever is underway in your backyard."

"I know what's good for you, Ida. Liver pills," Amelia said calmly. "Now pay up."

Ida glared at Amelia. "Or what? You'll shoot me?"

The druggist squeezed the slim glass bottle of pills in her hand. *Be nice,* she thought, but then said, "You might consider walking backward all the way to the door, Ida."

Ida snatched the pills from Amelia and slapped two coins on the counter. "Cravin's doesn't attract criminals."

Amelia just stared at her. Then, suddenly, she yelled, "Bang!"

Ida flinched and let out a small shriek. Looking irate, she twirled away from the counter, her long skirt swishing.

As Amelia watched Ida storm out of Polk's, she regretted shooting off her mouth.

But only for about two seconds.

Chapter 15

Yesterday, Boone had been guiding a powerful pair of horses to prepare soil for the tomato crop. Today, he was performing his tasks with limited horsepower. In fact, he had no horse at all—just Edison's mule, Byron, whose reins he'd dropped to the ground, having arrived at his destination. There was no need to bother with the hitching post. The old jack could barely pull a buckboard, let alone run off if left untethered. Boone then headed for Cravin & Company with a crate of grapefruit in his arms and a letter in his pocket. It had taken him a few weeks to follow through on what he'd discussed with Belle, but once he did, the words he'd written had come surprisingly easy. Perhaps Love had shimmied in beside Shame and coaxed it to move aside. After all, Love had big plans but couldn't realize them without a Larkin family reconciliation.

As Boone walked along Front Street, he thought through the words he'd shared with his folks:

Dear Ma and Pa,
I'm writing from Fort Myers in southwest Florida where I moved after leaving. I figured

some miles might be in order what with the terrible mistake I made. I can't imagine how angry you've been at me. But now I'm wondering . . . Can you forgive me? Can we be a family again? My address is on the envelope. I say a prayer for you and for Daniel each night. I hope God is still listening to me.

Your son, Boone

When he walked through the door of Cravin's, Boone smelled Ida before he saw her. The stench of her acrid perfume hung in the air. The snippy woman was standing behind the mail desk, her makeup appearing as ghostly as always—caked on white powder and clownish, overly rouged cheeks.

"You're behind on the fruit," Ida said without offering a greeting. "The Edisons deserve better, no?"

Boone set the crate on the counter with a thud. "Right. I'll have a word with the orchard, Ida," Boone replied, his tone flat.

She grunted and then went about preparing paperwork for the shipment, her veined hand moving a pencil across the form.

"Anything else?" she asked, looking past Boone, scanning the store.

Boone reached around to the back pocket of his dungarees. "I need to send this," he said, and held the letter out toward Ida.

She snatched the envelope and surveyed it, back and front. "Five cents," she said.

Boone dug out a nickel from his pocket and put it on the counter. "When will it go out?"

Ida adjusted her broad-brimmed hat, adorned with an enormous bow and a spray of white egret feathers. "Letters go out after two o'clock." She turned her back on Boone and began shuffling through a lopsided stack of mail.

He headed for the door without offering a goodbye. Once in the street, he took a deep breath. What might he gain from spending a total of five cents on a letter and four years away from his parents? He wanted more than just forgiveness. He wanted his family—what remained of it—back.

Boone gave Byron a pat on his bumpy backbone and then hopped up onto the seat of the buckboard. He'd done what he came to do. Now he simply had to wait and hope for the best.

• • •

The minute the screen door slammed, Ida began thinking through what she should write in a letter. She now had an address for Boone's family and a chance to expose the misguided leader of whatever crusade was currently underway to change Fort Myers for the worse. That disrespectful girl he courted—and her ilk—had already poisoned Hazel's mind and were now ginning up some sort of hysterical movement; Ida could feel it. A progressive fever was spiking and spreading. Even the pen in her hand seemed to heat up, ink dripping from its nib onto the blotter pad.

Ida disliked everything about Belle Carson: her sketchy upbringing, her undeserved connection to Mrs. Edison, her excessive free time with which to form silly clubs. Last year, members of the Circle Club—which Ida had *not* been invited to join—had embarrassed themselves by playing baseball. Hazel had looked ridiculous and promiscuous, and so attracted the attention of John Parker, his curiosity clearly piqued by the question of what else she might be willing to try. And now, something nefarious was underway involving young girls and pitchforks. Ida suspected progressive indoctrination disguised as gardening.

Breathing deeply, she closed her eyes and pictured her

deceased mother, Maxine. In the vision, she was pointing a knotty, bent finger at Ida. *A true woman is the moral protector of her husband and home,* she said, as she often had in life, her eyes narrowed. *Don't you ever doubt me, young lady.*

Ida nodded. Proper ladies did accept—not doubt—a life rooted in tradition. Yet her own daughter was questioning and defying the very norms that had guided generations of esteemed women. Hazel was disrespecting the Cravin name and risking her role as an elite pillar of the community.

It was not that Ida didn't understand temptation. As hard as she'd resisted it most of her life, she was keenly aware of the lure of free will. Even she had once been drawn in by the wild excitement of careening off the straight and narrow. What she'd done one afternoon—as a married woman—had been a moment of pure recklessness. Ida hung her head, remembering.

She'd been inside the Palms Hotel, delivering dry goods from Cravin's, when a young cow hunter looked at her in a way that startled, even astounded her. Men—including her husband in recent years—never gazed at her with desire. But this strapping man clearly did, and then he took matters one step further. His whispered invitation to join him upstairs had thrilled and enticed her. Like a stray cow, she'd wandered away from morality and fallen to her knees in a second-floor maintenance closet. The experience was heady and gamy and surreal. As she pleasured the man, his moans had sounded to her like, *Yes. Yes, you are beautiful and free.* She'd nearly felt the corset loosening around her hard-driving waist. Suddenly, his release was hers, too—release from decades of obeying rigid rules and absorbing maternal rants.

But when she caught a glimpse of the dirty mops and worn rags beside her, the waves of immense liberation were immediately overpowered by intense shame. Already on her knees, Ida had prayed for forgiveness from her heavenly Father. And from her mother. Maxine's daughter knew better, yet she'd allowed herself to abandon her responsibility as moral protector. How weak of her.

Since that dark day, Ida had recommitted herself to serving her husband and her community. She knew that high standards—like corsets—existed to maintain the ideal. Ida was certain that before long, Hazel and every woman involved in progressive pursuits would lament their race toward the modern and regret their selfish decisions. Eligible men—including John Parker—would run in the opposite direction once they realized their potential wives were "new" women, set on serving their own needs above all others.

"Enough . . . ," she said under her breath. She was determined to inform the Larkins of what type of woman was cavorting with their son.

After cleaning the ink off the tip of the pen, Ida pressed its steel point against a sheet of thick white paper and started to write.

Dear Mr. and Mrs. Larkin, she began.

Chapter 16

What she wanted to say to Merle was "I need to be back at Baker's in one hour," but instead Abigail stayed quiet and gripped the hard seat of the buckboard as it bounced along the bumpy streets of Fort Myers. She'd finally agreed to the "proper courting" Merle had been proposing for weeks. For Abigail, their transition to a romantic relationship had been going smoothly. Both she and Merle were still committed to work, and that's how she liked it—business as usual and personal time together now and then. The perfect combination.

But recently, Merle had begun talking about his desire for more togetherness to make up for lost time as a couple. He'd explained that he wanted to spoil her and shower her with romantic gestures like *nice long picnics*. Abigail had thought, *Oh no*, when he'd said it. She was not good at—nor fully interested in—lingering or lounging around. But she had accepted his offer with feigned enthusiasm and a kiss. Now she was sitting beside her suitor and holding tight to the basket full of food in her lap.

"Isn't this a fine afternoon, my gal?" Merle asked, his abundant teeth turned toward her in a broad smile. He was white-knuckling the leather reins attached to a young, feisty horse straining to turn the buckboard into a bullet.

Abigail nodded while imagining a sink full of dirty dishes at the boardinghouse. "It's just delightful, Squirrel."

Out of respect for Abigail's busy schedule, Merle had chosen a Wednesday for the big outing rather than a weekend, when the bulk of boarders arrived and departed. It was a kind but futile gesture. Wednesday meant nothing to ducks and chickens and gardens that required daily care, not to mention hungry patrons who needed attention seven days a week. How thankful she was to Grace Bailey, who'd agreed to manage as many tasks as she could while Abigail was . . . wherever.

"Mind telling me where we're headed?" Abigail asked, hoping they'd arrive somewhere soon. The terrain was even rougher out beyond the town limits.

Merle shook his head no and smiled. "The mystery adds to the fun, don't you think?"

Abigail didn't answer. *Thumpity-thump.* Her backside couldn't disagree more.

Because Merle had waited too long to secure their transportation, the rickety buckboard and eager Diablo had been the only options at the livery. In between holes in the road, Abigail was trying to convince herself that her and Merle's differences were a good thing—his last-minute spontaneity a balance to her detailed planning.

"Almost there . . . ," Merle said in a singsong tone, Diablo winning his battle for a speedy transit.

Soon, they were hurtling toward a weathered gray barn that was in relatively good shape—a few missing planks, a moss-covered roof, and a slight tilt to the left. Wide-eyed, Merle let out a *"Whoa!"* the sound more like a scream than a command, and pulled back on the reins until his arms shook. Abigail groaned and held the basket in front of her face, bracing for impact. Just a few feet from the barn, Merle somehow got Diablo to stop, sand exploding under the horse's skidding hooves.

The couple sat in stunned silence for a moment, then Merle got down and walked around the buckboard, hobbling a bit. "Let me help you, dear," he offered. She took his hand—and her time—climbing down. They'd both endured quite a ride.

The sweaty black colt munched on chicory as Merle poured water into a small bucket for the animal, its lips rimmed with white foam. Next, he unloaded picnic gear and escorted Abigail to a sandy patch next to the old barn. The broad canopy of a royal poinciana tree provided dappled shade below.

"I happened upon this place last month when I met up with my cigar man. He's out of Ybor City and travels all over the state peddling his Sanchez y Haya smokes." Merle moved a canteen hanging from his shoulder to the ground. "I met him here instead of in town because I can't let that slippery Ida Cravin see his truck. He's agreed to a Duggan's exclusive, but still . . ."

Abigail snapped the hem of a checked cloth blanket and let it drift down to the ground. "Smart, Squirrel. That woman would snatch a rainbow from the sky if she thought she could hawk it at Cravin's."

Merle put his hands on his hips. "All right, enough talk about work. I started it, but no more from here on out."

Swatting at a fly, she said, "We've always talked about work. Since the day we met."

"Not when we're spending special time together, we don't." He smiled. "New rule."

"What? Now there are rules?" She watched him set out the basket and a custom-built crate with compartments for silverware, plates, and glasses. "Who made you king, Duggan?"

"You did, when you became my queen," he said. "Now let's eat."

Standing next to the blanket, Abigail let out a short breath.

Her personal bulk made a picnic her least favorite way to eat a meal. She watched as lanky six-foot Merle sat down and splayed his long legs out in front of him. It wouldn't be so easy for her. Five foot tall and round, she'd be more comfortable lying sideways to eat. Still, she slowly bent her legs and plopped down with a thud onto her sore bottom.

Merle poured lemonade from the canteen into two etched glasses. He'd brought elegant china plates, too, but both had broken during the rough ride. Apologizing, Merle had explained that, despite Clay's superior workmanship, the custom-built crate had failed to protect its contents during the brutal bumping and thumping.

"Here you go," he said, handing Abigail a sandwich.

She could feel sweat beads sliding down her back, even as the day turned cloudy. Merle also looked hot but very happy. She dabbed her glistening upper lip with a napkin and examined her sandwich. Egg salad on sourdough, a combination new to her. She took a bite.

"How's the sandwich, honey?" Merle asked, holding one in front of his mouth.

She was encountering something crunchy, likely eggshells. She stopped chewing and took a small sip of lemonade, which proceeded to dribble down her chin through a fresh crack in the glass. She ignored the drip and forced herself to swallow, wondering whether to be polite about the shells or to save Merle from taking his own miserable bite.

Instead, she let out a shriek. *"Ow!"* Something was biting her ankles just above her boots. She dropped the sandwich and lifted the hem of her dress. "Fire ants!" she declared and flicked at the tiny bugs swarming her legs.

Merle crawled on his hands and knees to her. He grabbed a napkin and swiped away a line of reddish-brown ants on the march across the blanket.

"Well, blast it," he said, and stood to help Abigail up and away from the scene of the attack. "Are you okay?"

"Oh, Merle," Abigail said, wiping her sleeves in case of ants. "I love you, but what do you say we head back home. I'll make us lunch."

Merle sighed, pulled out his pocket watch, and checked it. "We can't. Not yet."

Abigail started to respond but then spotted two figures in the distance approaching on horseback.

"Who do we have here?" she said, peering at the horizon where black storm clouds were starting to bloom.

Merle's shoulders slumped and Abigail could see he was growing deflated. First the wild ride, then the busted dishes and biting bugs, and now, an important part of his special day was arriving on the heels of a storm. Right then, Abigail decided it was time to make some guidelines of her own.

"No getting soaked on our special days together," she said. "*My* new rule. Now, you lead Diablo and the buckboard into the barn. I'll gather up our picnic supplies and shake off that ant blanket."

She quickly and efficiently packed up the food and tableware and hustled inside the large structure, which still smelled like the hay it once housed. The air was cooler inside and several square windows provided substantial light, even with the darkening sky. Two oxbows hung from a rafter, the smaller missing one of its U-shaped collars. A climbing aster vine sneaking through the barn's siding was draped around stubby pegs where bridles and ropes may have previously hung. Cobwebs claimed every corner.

Abigail was pleased to see a long wooden table and four tree stumps set up along one wall. Clearly, other people used the abandoned barn to eat and seek shelter, too. Outside, thunder rumbled and rain would soon follow.

Once Merle had led Diablo into the barn and secured him, he said, "I'll be right back." He then headed outside, closing one of the barn's two large front doors, leaving the other open for whoever was arriving.

Abigail began resetting the picnic on the table, scratching at her swelling ant bites. She desperately wanted to go home, but first and foremost, she wanted to lift Merle's spirits. He truly was trying so hard to romance her.

For both their sakes she left the sandwiches in the basket and created a savory display from the crackers, guava jam, and cured sausages Merle had packed. She nibbled on dried fruit as she added it to the offerings. Outside, plump raindrops began to smack the sand and lightning flashed. Wind thrashed the poinciana's leaves and frenzied every palm frond in sight. As she poured what remained of the lemonade, Abigail heard snorting and the jingling of bridle hardware as horses shook their heads.

"C'mon in, gentlemen," Merle said. He appeared in the open doorway with Butch and Elliot Cooper. The twin brothers led their horses into the barn and greeted Abigail simultaneously.

"Boy, Merle sure has thought of everything," Butch said, looking around. "Nice and dry in here."

"He's . . . quite the planner," Abigail said, and then asked the brothers about their wives.

She noticed that the men were wearing tattered black suits and bowler hats, standard attire for the Fort Myers Band. Like Butch and Elliot, all members of the town band were volunteers and rarely practiced, too busy providing for their growing families. As a result, anyone who called their music *ethereal* must surely be tone-deaf. But that's exactly how Mina Edison had described it during her and her husband's 1885 honeymoon stay at Seminole Lodge. The phrase quoted in the *Press* had been "quite ethereal." That description was quite a stretch, but typical of the ever-gracious Mrs. Edison.

"Just two of us today," Elliot said. "Merle thought the whole band would be too much." He began to untie his violin case from the saddle. Butch did the same with his trumpet case. Diablo nickered at the other horses as the musicians watered and secured them. Rain hammered the roof and thunder shook the ground. Everyone stayed away from the windows.

"Honestly, two of you is two more than I expected." She glanced at Merle and added, "And what a truly wonderful surprise." Merle beamed and she gestured toward the table. "Are either of you hungry?"

"Oh no, thank you," Butch responded, and in unison the men declared, "We're on the job." They got busy moving a stump and stacking their instrument cases on it. They left the top case open to prop up their sheet music.

Merle and Abigail sat down at the table, and as Merle slid his arm around her, a drip hit the top of her bun. A moment later, another trickled down her forehead.

"How about we slide over to the other stumps," she suggested softly.

After they did, the twins turned toward each other. Abigail thought they must feel as if they were looking in a mirror. They gave each other a quick nod of support, then turned back to face their audience of two.

Next, Elliot began tuning his violin, a screechy, high-pitched process. After a minute passed, Abigail realized that he was in fact playing a song, and soon Butch joined in on the trumpet. The pair sounded better together, but still, it seemed as if the staff had tilted sideways on the score, notes crashing into each other as they slid off the page. The cacophony raged on right along with the storm, which seemed to join in—the crack of lightning as cymbals, thunder a bass drum.

When the bungled but well-intended duet finally ended, Merle and Abigail showered them with praise. The men bowed, tipping their hats on the way back to upright.

"Gentlemen, this has been unlike any picnic I've ever attended," Abigail said, slapping her thighs. She turned toward Merle. "And this has been our best special day together yet." She gently placed her hands on his graying beard and pulled his face down to hers. "But my bottom will never forgive you."

He said softly, "We'll see about that . . ."

She kissed him tenderly while slipping her arms around his neck. Maybe young love was more enchanting and graceful, but she wouldn't trade it for the seasoned, deep connection she shared with this dear man—eggshells and all.

Chapter 17

On his walk to Blevins Park, Boone recalled Abigail's amusing recounting of yesterday's outing with Merle and its series of foibles. He'd asked her about it when he noticed her hobbling around the garden after being "properly courted" earlier in the day.

"Had an alligator crawled out from the brush and eaten us both, I wouldn't have been surprised!" she'd declared, her outstretched arms clamping open and shut in a chomping motion.

Still, despite all the glitches, he could tell by Abigail's beaming face that she was touched by Merle's valiant effort to woo her. Boone let his mind wander for a bit longer, but when he finally arrived at the park, he turned his focus to the task at hand. The time had come to hear from the other end of the olive branch.

He chose a long bench flanked by two cabbage palms and sat down to read the letter that had arrived this afternoon, nearly two weeks after he'd written to his parents. Ida had walked out from behind the mail desk to hand him the letter. "Looks like someone wrote you from Kissimmee," she'd said, staring intensely at the letter, as if her curiosity might somehow draw out its contents.

Examining the envelope, Boone noted that his mother had addressed it. Her familiar handwriting was a comforting sight. He hoped her words would be, too.

He sliced open the envelope with a pocketknife and pulled out the paper inside. When he unfolded it, he saw a brief note.

> *Boone,*
>
> *We didn't know where you were. Thank God you're all right. Now come home immediately and clean up the other mess you left behind.*

Boone blinked down at the note, stunned. His mother's words were confusing and curt. What was this "other mess"? Something more than the cow camp tragedy? Boone set the letter down on the bench and slowly rubbed his temples. Time away had not healed anything back home. In fact, something of his doing—other than Daniel's death—had been festering in his absence. *Come home.*

Reeling, Boone decided right then and there he couldn't bear writing or waiting for any more letters. He had to see his ma and pa in person. Decker would just have to manage without him for a while. Until he fully understood the circumstances, Boone would simply tell Belle that his trip to Kissimmee was a solid first step in rebuilding his relationship with his parents. He needed to understand the mess himself before sharing anything about it with her. But, before he left for home, there was something very important he needed to do.

• • •

Belle was examining rows in the tomato patch when Boone caught up with her. The girls were in school, but several days earlier they'd transplanted seeds sown in boxes into the large field.

"Our plants are now six to seven inches," Belle reported after kissing him. "They're doing well in the grown-up patch." She paused and looked him up and down. "You look nice."

Boone's heart was pounding as if she'd just told him she'd found a gold nugget under one of the plants. Her beautiful smile with the cute little gap in her front teeth was something he wanted to treasure forever. He simply could not lose this remarkable woman.

"Well . . . I'm going home to Kissimmee for a little while." He took her hands in his, hoping she wouldn't feel them shaking.

"Oh, Boone, did you hear from your parents?" She laced her fingers through his.

"I sure did, and they want to see me," he said, forcing a smile.

"That's wonderful," she responded, bouncing with excitement. "When do you leave?"

"A day or two," he said. "I've got to break it to Decker, who'll be madder than an old wet hen."

"Oh, I'll handle Decker," Belle said. "Mr. Ritter should be able to fill in some. He has plenty of help at the sawmill."

"I hope he can," Boone said. He paused and gathered himself. "There is one thing you can do for me, Belle." He gazed at her face—tanned skin, almond eyes, full lips. Her wavy hair was wrangled into a loose bun, a pencil holding it in place.

"Anything, love," she said.

Slowly, he lowered his large frame toward the ground and fell to one knee. Belle's hands flew to her mouth as he reached into his shirt pocket. Boone certainly recognized the absurdity of proposing in a tomato patch, but that didn't stop him.

"Belle, you're an answer to a prayer I didn't even make. I knew I was broken but never thought I deserved to be put back together." He paused and tried to think of something more to say, something about gardening. Instead, he took her left hand and unfolded his, revealing a makeshift ring.

A single tear trickled down Belle's cheek. "Boone . . ."

He held up the improvised trinket. "Someday, I'll get you a proper ring, but for right now . . . I hope you'll accept this."

She wiped the tear away and then wiggled her fingers at the right-now ring: a circle of wire threaded through two holes of an ivory button. "Put it on me," she said.

He chuckled. "Is that a 'yes'?"

"Yes!" she exclaimed. Jumping with excitement, she shouted, "Did you hear that, tomatoes? I said yes!" She helped him push the ring onto her finger and then wrapped her arms around his neck when he stood up.

"Oh, Boone," she whispered in his ear. "This is just perfect."

He laughed. "Only you would think a proposal made standing in compost was perfect." He kissed her. "Just one of many reasons I love you."

"And I love you and my special ring," she said, taking a long look at her hand, which she held out flat. "My dirty fingernails have never looked better."

Boone drew Belle in and kissed her for as long as she let him. His journey home now seemed a little less daunting.

Chapter 18

Many of the pages in Abigail's *Dixie Cook-Book,* 1885 revised edition, were splattered with stains from various liquids that had been required for recipes carried out in her kitchen—beef broth, vanilla, vinegar. On the center of page 345, pink splash marks smudged the instructions for making Sweet Pickled Beets. But, this afternoon, Abigail and the Dawson girls were not interested in beets. Right below the pickling recipe was a contribution by Mrs. S. Watson: directions for making Tomato Toast, the recipe Fae had chosen.

"Mazie, start assembling your ingredients so you'll be ready when we move on to your dish," Abigail directed.

Both girls busied themselves gathering spices and cooking tools, setting up on whatever counter space they could find in the organized but busy Baker kitchen. Abigail had just served lunch to several boarders while the girls picked tomatoes in her vegetable garden, their leafing shoots having just recently been transplanted at Polk's. The club literature Virginia had sent encouraged tomato girls to test their recipes before adding them to their booklets, so Abigail had volunteered to oversee the process. Belle and the other Circle Club members were busy with work or family, and Abigail was delighted to help the girls, who'd walked over to Baker's after school.

"I wonder why Mrs. Watson was making tea while she cooked," Mazie said, retying her apron strings behind her back. "You told us we shouldn't daydream or get distracted while we cook, Miss Abigail."

Abigail chuckled. "How do you know she was making tea?" She finished drying the last of the lunch dishes and began returning them to cupboards and shelves.

Mazie ran her finger along the words in the cookbook as she read. "'Just as the bell rings for tea, add a pint of good sweet cream to the stewed tomatoes, and pour them over toast.'"

Fae stopped slicing bread and pointed her long knife at Mazie. "Stop reading ahead. I'm not to that part yet." Fae's prepared tomato mixture was stewing in a pot on the stove.

Just then, two boarders entered the kitchen. A woman carrying a tackle box smiled at the girls and Abigail. "I thought too many cooks spoiled the broth," she said, her tone cheerful.

The man behind her lightly tapped her on the bottom with the tip of his fishing pole. "Let's let these ladies do their work."

Mazie smiled back at the woman and patted her hand on the open cookbook. "We're recipe testers."

"Oh, you are?" the woman exclaimed. "Isn't that wonderful, Dennis?"

Dennis was obviously eager to exit Baker's. "*We're* about to test the waters for redfish. C'mon, darlin'."

"Oh, good luck to us all, then!" the woman declared, offering a fluttery finger wave as the couple left the kitchen through the screen door.

"Mazie, please read Fae's recipe out loud from the start," Abigail said, and hung the damp dish towel on the stove handle to dry.

"And do it slowly," Fae commanded her younger sister.

Mazie began. "'Tomato Toast. Run a quart of stewed ripe

tomatoes through a colander, place in a porcelain stew-pan, season with butter, pepper and salt, and sugar to taste. Cut slices of bread thin, brown on both sides, and butter and lay on a platter. Just as the bell rings for tea, add a pint of good sweet cream to the stewed tomatoes, and pour them over toast. Mrs. S. Watson.'" She looked up from the book. "Done yet, Sissy?"

Abigail spoke before Fae could snap at her sister. "I've never made this recipe before either, so we're learning together, ladies. Fae, are your stewed tomatoes done?"

Fae moved away from her bread and lifted the lid on the simmering pot. "They look beaten to a pulp." She looked over at Abigail. "Is that done?"

"Yes, honey, but taste it now to check the seasoning," Abigail instructed. Earlier, she'd helped Fae add sugar, salt and pepper, onions, basil, and bell peppers to the skinned tomatoes. She'd explained that bacon fat left over from breakfast—in place of Mrs. Watson's butter—would add a smoky flavor to the mix.

Fae dipped a spoon into the pot and then blew on the steaming tomatoes. After a taste, she said, "Mmm. Good idea on the bacon, Miss Abigail."

"Just one example of how the kitchen can be a wonderful place to experiment and be creative," Abigail said.

Sharing time with these young girls reminded her of when Belle used to come over to cook, when she was just a few years older than the Dawsons. As a teenager, Belle had been more comfortable in a garden than a kitchen, but she'd seemed to enjoy learning how to use a mortar and pestle or roll pie dough. She'd clearly relished gobbling up whatever dish they'd prepared, strawberry shortcake being her favorite. Abigail had also taught Belle skills related to cooking, like how to preserve fresh eggs in limewater. And how to render and strain lard.

"Did you girls know that Miss Belle used to cook with me when she was just a few years older than you?" Abigail said, wanting to share the memory. She handed Fae's notebook to her. "Write down the recipe instructions so far for the toast so you don't forget what you've done."

Fae took the notebook and slid a pencil out from behind her ear. "Why didn't Miss Belle's mother teach her how to cook?"

Abigail blinked at the girl. She hadn't expected that response. As Fae began to write in her notebook and Mazie measured salt into a small bowl, Abigail considered how to answer. The story of Belle's mother—or rather, her natural mother and her adoptive one—was complicated. She recalled what Merle had shared with her many years ago about Eva Logan.

In 1862, Clara Burns, whom Merle was then engaged to, had served as a midwife in Fort Myers. One day she'd been called upon to assist a nineteen-year-old single woman named Eva who was giving birth on nearby Sanibel Island. Eva had lost her parents to a fire in Punta Rassa the year prior and subsequently was tricked into serving as a parlor girl at the port town's Sandy Spur Hotel.

After she became pregnant, Eva had left the Spur and taken the mail boat *Spitfire* to Sanibel to find a castor bean farmer named Arthur who'd mentioned, while in Punta Rassa, that he'd needed help with his crop on the island. Scared and in desperate circumstances, Eva had decided to ask Arthur for a job. She needed a roof over her head and a safe place to map out her future. Arthur had hired her and after months working on the bean farm, Eva's original plan to find a good home for the baby had changed. She'd told Arthur that she wanted to keep her child.

But when Eva went into labor, complications had developed quickly. As the teen struggled, the frantic farmer begged the mail boat captain to find a way to get a midwife out to the island. Sadly, by the time Clara arrived, Eva had already lost too much blood. Clara was only able to save the baby.

Devastated, Arthur had helped rush Clara and her bundle to the waiting boat.

Baby and midwife endured a stormy sail back to Fort Myers aboard the *Maybelle*, which Clara named the little girl after in honor of the trusty boat. Merle and Clara quickly agreed that they would adopt Belle, but then tragedy struck again. One week after she'd returned from Sanibel, Clara was bitten by a rattler and died. It would be another fourteen years before Belle found her way to Merle, and to Abigail, and after the pair welcomed her into their loving arms, the new arrangement proved an unexpected and immeasurable blessing for all three of them.

"Unfortunately, Miss Belle's mother died giving birth to her," was all Abigail said to Fae and Mazie. "So I was happy to teach her about cooking. The Baileys taught her about plants and gardening."

Abigail knew Belle wouldn't mind her telling the girls about her mother's death. In fact, Belle had said she'd hoped her loss might help her lend a loving ear to the girls should they ever need one.

Mazie walked over to Abigail, holding a measuring spoon full of pepper. "Does that make you Miss Belle's mother?"

Abigail placed her palm on Mazie's cheek. "No, but we *are* family."

Fae was browning slices of bread in a skillet. "Poor Miss Belle. She never got to meet her mother."

Abigail moved away from Mazie and toward the stove. She handed Fae a plate with a hunk of butter on it. "No, she didn't. But Eva is an angel who watches over Belle, just like your mother and father watch over you. Parents never stop protecting their children."

"I hope that's true," Fae said softly, and began to butter her slices of toasted bread. "Mazie, will you add the sweet cream to my tomatoes?"

"Of course, Sissy," Mazie said, and grabbed a glass bottle off the counter. When she got to the stove, she wrapped her arm around Fae's waist and poured cream into the pot, turning the sauce pink. "I sure do like cooking with family."

Fae looked down at her sister and smiled.

Abigail draped her arms across both girls' shoulders. "I sure do, too," she said, and kissed them each on top of their heads.

Chapter 19

Boone hadn't traveled in a passenger car since he rode the Florida Southern Railway nearly four years ago southwest to Fort Myers. Now, on this overcast Sunday, his journey back home via boat and train was nearly complete. He'd spent the first part of the rail trip writing a letter to Belle, and now the final stretch recalling his life in Kissimmee before the terrible accident. Back then, his days and weeks had been as predictable as the gingerbread clock in the Larkins' humble home. His mother kept the family fed and faithful, and his father managed the herd, constantly directing Daniel and Boone to the places where scrub cattle were straying in the palmetto-laden underbrush. Sometimes the trio camped in the wooded rangelands for several days, but Sunday church was not to be missed.

"We worship the Lord in this family, not cows," his mother would affirm.

Boone and Daniel had rarely fought, and instead worked hard to complete their chores so they'd have time to chase women, not just strays. Daniel had never pursued just one woman, appearing content to chat up whichever gal might interest him in the moment. Respectful and kind, he easily charmed the ladies, but never one Boone had eyes for. Tilly Brown, who worked at the Tropical Hotel, was the only woman Boone had spent significant time with, the two of them sharing horseback rides and the occasional picnic. He'd enjoyed Tilly's company, but she'd been the furthest thing from his mind when he escaped Kissimmee years ago.

After the train finally braked to a stop, Boone stretched his legs and exited the railcar in front of the long wooden station, a covered porch jutting out from one side. The post office was still operating out of the facility, so he mailed his letter to Belle. The depot hadn't changed a bit, but so much in his life had. Dressed in freshly laundered clothes, he shouldered a small bag and one big question: *What is this "other mess" I've left behind?*

As he walked from the depot toward his house, Boone recalled a family tradition that he and Daniel had pretended to endure but secretly enjoyed—at least he had. Many Sundays after church, when they got home, his mother would play the piano and sing songs. Whenever they went into town to shop at Makinson & Katz, she always bought new sheet music if it was available. His mother was a good piano player and an even better singer, her strong voice belying her slight frame. While she played, his father would read the *Old Farmer's Almanac* and Daniel would whittle, but Boone just sat and listened, the four of them gathered in the Larkins' small but comfortable back room.

Suddenly, a song tugged at his memory. He began to sing it softly as he walked.

"'Do not let your chances like sunbeams pass you by, for you never miss the water till the well runs dry.'" He hummed through all the words he'd forgotten but was surprised by how many he remembered. "'We have little children three, hmm-mm-mm, I teach them as they prattle on my knee.'" And then he sang the chorus again as he moved closer and closer to home.

When Boone arrived at his house, no one was in the yard. The familiar canoe garden filled with herbs was still nestled in its place among a pile of river rocks, mint spilling out over the bowed wooden sides. During his absence, someone had hung a wagon wheel horizontally from a thick branch of their gumbo-limbo tree to create a swing. Boone walked past both and right through the front door, bracing for the unknown.

"Hello?" he called from the front hall.

"Back here," his father answered from the kitchen.

Boone entered the room and stared at the scene before him. His parents were seated at the table, set for three. Sunday dinner was laid out before them on wide platters and inside steaming crocks. A plump ham dotted with cloves filled the air with a familiar porky scent.

"Um, hello," Boone said, slowly setting his bag down on the floor.

Boone's mother twisted around on a bench that ran the length of the table. "You got my letter," she said, releasing an audible sigh.

Boone looked back and forth between his mother and father. Both appeared the same, but his memory of the time following the accident was questionable. After Daniel's death, he and his parents had become a trio of shadows, distorted and stretched thin with pain. At least the dark circles under his mother's eyes had faded.

"Did you get *my* letter?" Boone asked, wondering if he should sit down in front of the empty plate.

"We got *a* letter," his mother answered. "It laid out your doings with a reckless woman trying to whip things up in your town."

"What?" Boone said quietly. "Who would write you a letter about me and . . . ?"

His mother interrupted. "Wasn't signed, but it had a Fort Myers postmark."

Before Boone could ask any more questions, a female voice floated in from the hallway. "We're here, Nana and Paw Paw."

A woman Boone's age walked into the kitchen alongside a child carrying a plate heaped with something under a cloth napkin. The brunette stopped in her tracks when she saw Boone.

"Tilly?" Boone asked, and then glanced over at the child.

The woman's face paled, but she directed the boy toward the table without missing a beat. He sat down on the bench and placed his food in front of him.

"Wyatt doesn't like ham, but he likes everything else," she explained while removing the napkin. "So we bring an extra plate of roasted chicken for him. It's a Sunday tradition."

Boone's face must have conveyed his confusion, but his father only said, "Go grab a chair, boy."

Boone wandered into the next room, relieved for the chance to catch his breath. Tilly was in the kitchen . . . with a child. *Nana and Paw Paw?* Was this "the mess"? It certainly wasn't his mess. He took a deep breath and picked up a chair.

Once they were all seated around the table, no one offered to get Boone a plate. He was starving, so he got up and walked to the cupboards. He had to open several doors to locate the dishware because several things in the kitchen had been rearranged since he'd left. The gingerbread clock now sat on the counter instead of the corner cabinet.

"This is Wyatt," Tilly said, caressing the boy's blond curls as he wolfed down his dinner.

"Uh. Nice to meet you, Wyatt," Boone said, too far away to offer the boy his hand.

Wyatt stopped eating long enough to say, "I'm four." He then resumed devouring a drumstick.

Everyone ate quietly for a few minutes, forks clinking and tea pouring the only sounds in the room.

"Wyatt, go out and play on the swing Paw Paw made for

you, all right?" Tilly said, breaking the silence once the child had polished off his chicken.

Wyatt left the table, grabbing a handful of coconut pralines on his way out.

Boone cleared his throat. "What are you doing here, Tilly?"

His father spoke first. "Remember Tilly? Your sweetheart?"

"C'mon, Pa. We weren't serious," Boone said, and pushed away his empty plate.

His mother slammed her fists on the table, startling everyone. "You left behind your father and me, and Tilly, and now you see . . ." She was pointing her finger at Boone. "You abandoned a son, too."

Tilly nodded, her features pinched, as if preparing for tears.

Boone vigorously shook his head. "No, no . . . no. That's impossible."

Tilly started to cry. "You left us," she said, sniffling as she spoke. "After what you and I did . . . to me it was *very* serious."

His father was glaring at him. "Reckless with our family and reckless with your manhood," he spat.

Boone stood up from his chair. "I will *not* allow this. I'll take responsibility for . . . some things. But Tilly"—he turned to her—"you know a child for us is impossible."

His father gestured across the table. "You saw the child, Son!"

Now his mother was crying into her napkin. Boone persisted. "Tilly, you and I never did that . . . sort of thing. And you know it."

Tilly got up and blew her nose. "I need to check on Wyatt," she whimpered, and left the house.

Boone pleaded with his parents. "You have got to believe me. That is *not* my child." His fists were clenched.

"You've got a lot of nerve," his father said. "Lying to us and now breaking your mother's heart . . . again." He got up. "I've got to cool down," he said, striding into the dining room.

Boone slowly sat down next to his mother. "I swear, Wyatt is not my son."

His mother cried harder and then slowly quieted. "He looks just like you."

Boone sighed. "Tilly and I were never . . . intimate, Ma. At the time Daniel died, she and I were spending time together, but not . . ."

His mother held up her hand. "Enough. Tilly says otherwise."

Boone rested his head in his hands. "Ma, I came here to repair things with you and Pa." He breathed in deeply, then looked back up at his mother. "I'm in love with a gal in Fort Myers, and I can't start a life with her if things here aren't right."

His mother's eyes flashed with anger. "You selfish boy. Your life is here . . . with your son and Tilly."

Boone shook his head. "I don't know what Tilly is trying to do—maybe she's scared—but she's got you and Pa fooled." He reached over and touched his mother's hand. She started to pull it away but then left it, allowing his gesture.

"You should know, Boone, Tilly is hurting," she insisted. "You left her here alone to raise your boy. Pa and I have done all we can to help, but now it's time for you to be a father."

Boone groaned. He lifted himself up and off the bench. "I need some air, too."

• • •

Tilly was pushing Wyatt on the wagon-wheel swing when he walked outside. The boy was giggling, both arms stretched toward the sky, which must have seemed to him to be in reach. Boone was still in shock as he approached the pair.

"Look, Tilly," he said. "You're going to have to come clean with my parents."

Tilly offered one last push of the swing. "I'll be right over here, Wy," she said, and waved Boone toward the other side of the yard.

When they were in a secluded spot, Tilly grabbed Boone's shirt, pulled him to her, and kissed him. Immediately, he pushed her away.

"Stop it, Tilly. You're not my girl," he said. Her thin lips felt unfamiliar and unwelcome. Only Belle's lips fit his perfectly. "I'm in love with someone else."

Tilly slammed her palms against his chest and shoved him backward. "You don't get to be happy, Boone. You have a child to take care of . . . here, with me."

Boone moved back closer to her and clenched his jaw. "What cowboy did you bed, Tilly? Couldn't get him to stick around?"

Her eyes flashed and then narrowed. "You'd better hush, Boone. I know what you did," she said with a slight grin.

"What are you talking about?" Boone demanded, irked by her sly look. It wasn't a secret—at least not in his family—that he was responsible for Daniel's death. He hadn't considered until now that his parents would tell anyone. Just how much did Tilly know?

"Wyatt is yours and you just let that sink in," she said, flipping her long brown hair off her shoulders.

Boone looked over at Wyatt, now sitting upright on the swing, singing to himself. "You don't know anything, Tilly. You're not a part of this family."

"Oh, I don't know about that," Tilly said. "Your mother was wrecked after Daniel died. There was a lot of gossip in town. No funeral, no real answers about what happened to your brother." She smirked at Boone. "Nana . . . well, she needed an ear."

Boone grabbed her arm. He wanted to yank it, to jerk the truth out of the girl. But he didn't. "Don't you call her *Nana*. You're not related to her and neither is that boy."

Tilly easily shrugged her arm loose from Boone's light grip. "You best be nicer to me." She began to walk away toward Wyatt but said over her shoulder, "Our sheriff has a jail now . . . if you haven't heard."

Chapter 20

Belle hadn't been apart from Boone this long—more than a week now—since they'd met. Back in the spring, he'd been gone for a few days when he took Byron upriver to the town of Olga, where a veterinarian specialized in mule care. Byron had devoured some of the feed sack Boone accidentally left in the swayback's livery stable and became ill. Knowing thrifty Mr. Edison would just as soon let the feeble animal die—Byron ate more than he worked—Boone had paid the vet and boarding-house fees himself. Since that trip, Belle and Boone had seen each other nearly every day.

Now she was tidying up his sailboat, anchored beside the Edisons' long wooden wharf. Boone had told her the *Judith* was named after a beloved horse he rode during his cowboy days in Kissimmee, and she thought about his tender heart as she dusted belowdecks. The two of them often talked and shared long kisses here in his private hideaway. Boone would slowly free her long hair from its braid or feed her sections of an orange as she lay stretched across his lap.

When candlelit, the small space always seemed romantic to her despite its minimal decor. An old captain's wheel was affixed to a post, and Boone's canteen hung from one of its spindles. A long, narrow sculling oar was secured horizontally over his bed, and stacked circles of ropes lay at its foot. Today, a hollowed-out cypress burl held several pieces of fruit, including a molded orange and two brown bananas. Surely, Boone had been preoccupied before he left and that's why the fruit remained in the bowl. Or maybe he'd thought he would return home before anything could spoil. Either way, she'd remove it for him.

Belle lightly hummed as she swept the tiny room. Her body barely swayed on the boat this afternoon, the river beneath it calm. As she ran a straw broom far under the bed frame, it met with an object midsweep. Surprised, Belle dropped to her knees and looked to see what she'd hit. A bag of dirty laundry? It appeared to be a cloth sack full of something. Belle grabbed it and yanked it out in front of her. Reluctantly, she stuck her nose near the opening and took a quick whiff. Thankfully, there was no odor, but now she wondered what was inside.

"Hmm . . ." Belle stood and considered the sack on the ground. Certainly, she should respect Boone's privacy. The bag was probably hidden under the bed for a reason. Besides, how would she feel if he decided to snoop around her cottage? She wouldn't like it. Standing, she used a bootheel to start scooting the sack back under the bed. But then she stopped, still tempted. *What's in there?* Curiosity quickly found a way to justify the violation. "Maybe it's something I can help him with," she said, convincing herself and then sitting down on the bed.

She began to pull things from the sack and put them down beside her. There was a worn leather belt, several frayed bandannas, a pressed-tin match safe, and a cigar box with "El Principe de Gales" stamped on the top. She surveyed the stash. What did these items mean to Boone? Why would he put them under the bed?

The collection appeared unremarkable . . . until she opened the lid of the wooden box. Instead of cigars, a stack of folded notes was inside, tied up with a yellow hair ribbon. "Oh my," Belle whispered and closed the lid. She stared at the box and wished she'd found plump stogies inside instead. Whatever these letters were, they were so special to Boone that he'd saved them—and hid them. She drummed her fingers on the lid, deciding. She had no right to read the notes, but how could she not? Boone hadn't mentioned ever having had a serious partner, just a girl he'd liked and spent a little time with in Kissimmee, but he'd left her behind when he moved away. Boone was hers now. They were engaged, and the love she shared with him felt genuine and powerful. But still . . .

"I'm sorry, Boone," she said softly, and reopened the box. Gently, she pulled on both ends of the yellow silk, making sure to study exactly how the bow was tied. She selected the note on top and took a deep breath as she unfolded it. Her heart sank when she saw that the handwriting inside was cursive, the *i*'s dotted with tiny hearts. Clearly, a smitten woman had penned them. She read the first line:

> *To my Roo—*
> "Roo?" Belle said aloud, confused. "Who's Roo?"
> She kept reading.
> *I can't stop thinking about our time in the loft. Do you think we kept the cows up?*
> *Yours, T*

Belle squinted down at the note, trying to make sense of who these people were. This T's implication was far from cryptic. She unfolded the next note.

> *To my Roo—*
> *My fingers miss running through those gorgeous blond curls of yours. Not to mention other places.*

So, Roo was definitely Boone! His curls *were* gorgeous. Next note.

> *To my Roo—*
> *Let's splash around again in the Little Buck. I can't walk by that creek without thinking of you know what.*

Belle wanted to stop reading but couldn't. She read the spicy notes until she nearly *Roo*-ed herself sick. Was Boone playing around in a loft or a creek with T at that very moment? Did he have unfinished business with both his parents *and* the ribbon girl? She wondered if he'd kept the notes so he could relive the steamy encounters. After all, keeping cows awake was not part of *their* relationship. Yet Boone had seemed to respect her wish to be married before engaging in anything so intimate. She shook her head, mad at herself for prying, angry at Boone for saving T's naughty notes.

One last letter remained. Belle snapped it open, annoyed.

> *To my Roo—*
> *I want to marry you and I hope our little one has your blue eyes.*

Belle's hand flew to her face, covering her mouth. Her body stiffened, but her eyes flew back and forth over the sentence—"our little one." A child? *Boone has a child?!*

Suddenly her stomach began to churn, as if the boat were bucking on whitecaps. Just seconds earlier, she'd been sure the bond she shared with Boone was as strong as his leather cow whip. Frantically, she began to check each note for a date, but there were none. Could Boone have abandoned a son or daughter back home years ago? Maybe he'd lied about the reason he moved away. Was his brother in fact alive?

Troubling thoughts buzzed in her mind like a swarm of horseflies. She looked around the room. That oar hanging over his bed sure could cause a lot of damage. She resisted the urge to grab it and swing it around, destroying everything that was special to Boone. She chewed on her nail, glaring at the oar. *Oh no.* Now God would never hear her prayer. There would be no second chance at a child. Boone and his secrets had ruined everything.

Belle stood up, numb. The notes in her lap fluttered to the floor. The ring on her finger now meant nothing. Now it was just a silly old button and some wire. Distraught, she wriggled it off and chucked it into the wooden bowl with everything else that was rotten.

Chapter 21

Days later, Fae and Mazie stood side by side outside Polk's, surrounded by busy helpers Amelia, Sadie, and Hazel. Next to them, the remaining members of the Circle Club were sampling snacks spread across the picnic table positioned near the tomato field. Abigail had dropped off some of her most scrumptious offerings to date—apple custard pies, pickled eggs, fried codfish balls, and tea with lemon syrup.

"I think a fancy hem on your uniforms would be grand, don't you?" Amelia asked, glancing up at the girls from her kneeling position.

"Just please don't stick me," Fae said, standing very still. Amelia was using straight pins to attach a scalloped border to her dress.

Sadie was working on Fae's hair, straight and blonde. "Your pigtails are lopsided, honey. I'm gonna have to start again on the right side."

Alice popped up from her seat at the table, a half-eaten fish ball in her hand. "Why not leave it off-kilter, Sadie? Perfect is so boring." She tossed the cod into the air and caught it in her mouth.

Both girls bounced up and down with delight. In unison, Amelia and Sadie said, "Stand still!"

Hazel was focused on Mazie, creating a French braid in her hair as brown as a coffee bean. As she wove a green silk ribbon into the pretty plaits, she said, "We'll save the red ribbon for your booklet, Mazie, okay?"

"Yes. I want the longest, reddest ribbon for *my* booklet," Mazie answered.

Fae shook her head. "I guess Cotton Ears didn't hear Miss Belle's lesson about behaving like a team."

Before Mazie could offer a retort, Alice began performing cartwheels in front of the group. The distraction worked, and everyone stayed on task, preparing for the upcoming competition.

• • •

Belle was out in the field trying hard to stay focused on the maturing plants, but she was failing. Her thoughts kept drifting back to her horrible discovery on Boone's boat. Angrily, she dragged a hoe across weeds, cutting their leaves and stems away from the root. Thank goodness she'd kept the news of Boone's proposal to herself! They'd agreed to stay quiet about it until he returned from Kissimmee so they could share the good news together. But now there was only bad news. No marriage, no baby, no more believing that a long-lasting love was within reach for her.

She stopped working briefly and looked over at the club members, a half-hearted attempt to be grateful. Yes, she was blessed with people who loved her, and she them. And Merle and Abigail were angels in her life. But a relationship with a partner, a secret keeper, a protector . . . all of that was over.

"Stupid me," she whispered.

She stopped trying to be positive and allowed herself to

fume. She imagined Despair wrestling Gratitude to the ground and shoving its stupid tranquil face into the dirt. Deflated, she let the hoe drop to the ground and sat next to it, hugging her knees. Betrayal was such a devious magician. As if with the *poof* of a wand, all her insecurities had reappeared. She was an outsider again. A smelly orphan with no voice, invisible to those with the power to protect her. How had she ever come to finally believe that she deserved—or could sustain—a romantic relationship? So much had been stolen from her *before* she could choose it.

Last year, dreadful Julius—in town from Tampa—had tracked her down in the cottage and assaulted her in bed. In pain and a state of delirium, she'd stabbed him repeatedly, every jab to his neck a failed attempt to undo both what he'd just done to her and their twisted past. She'd managed to kill him, but he'd lived on in the form of a baby inside her.

Desperate after realizing her agonizing situation, she'd drunk countless cups of herbal tea, hoping to stop the pregnancy. By her actions—or by the grace of God—she'd had a miscarriage, another terrifying and painful experience. Broken and vulnerable, Belle had turned to Boone for support after both ordeals. They'd been there for each other as they healed from tragedies, and they'd fallen deeply in love. But now the man she'd believed was her warrior had betrayed and deceived her. Once again, she was damaged and abandoned. *Poof.*

Belle reached for weeds growing near where she sat, ripping them from the soil and tossing them into a messy pile. As her mind churned, she grabbed handfuls of chickweed and dandelions, tugging at the invaders. Then she crawled on her hands and knees through several rows, attacking quack grass and yanking on stubborn pigweed until its roots gave way.

"Belle . . . ," a voice said. A hand touched her back, startling her. "Take a break, dear."

Belle turned and sat upright. "Oh, hello, Poppy." She tried

to catch her breath and wiped off her dirty hands on her dress. "I guess I got a little carried away."

"It's understandable, honey," Poppy said. "We all want the girls to succeed." She handed Belle a glass of sweet tea. "Drink this."

Belle took several swigs of the lemony tea as Poppy pulled a letter from her dress pocket. "Abigail sent this along with the refreshments. It's for you . . . from Kissimmee."

Belle said nothing and toyed with the weed pile next to her, trying to calm herself.

"She said Boone is in Kissimmee visiting his parents," Poppy continued.

"He is," Belle said. She'd told Abigail and Merle that Boone made the journey because he hadn't been back home in so long. A truth—but not the whole story. Up until now, she'd believed the omission about family trouble should be their business as a loving couple, but that was before Deceit had shown up, wrapped in a ribbon.

Poppy drew the letter back when Belle didn't take it. "Are you all right, dear?"

Belle could have told Poppy what was eating at her. A pastor's wife, Poppy was exceptional at keeping people's sufferings to herself, and many in the community relied upon her compassionate ear and steadfast discretion. Still, Belle had no intention of sharing her pain with Poppy, or with anyone. Saying the words out loud would gut her. Better to tear the heads off weeds right now.

"I'm fine. Thanks for delivering this, Poppy," Belle said. She reached out, took the letter, and flipped it over, interested in only one thing.

The return address.

Chapter 22

Town Marshal David Bass acknowledged that he'd never had a man voluntarily check himself in for detention. But this morning, before he'd even drunk his coffee, Boone had changed that.

"I hope you know what you're doing, son," Bass said, now standing outside the cell where Boone was resting. He worked a toothpick hanging from his mouth, rotating it with his tongue. "Nobody's here to represent you." Bass was filling in for the sheriff, who was away on extended business.

"It's the right thing to do, sir," Boone said, stretched out on a hard cot.

A courthouse and jail were still under construction in Kissimmee, so Osceola County allowed peace officers like the marshal to house prisoners at the sheriff's office, and that was where Boone had turned himself in for killing his brother.

The tubby marshal walked closer and grabbed the bars with both hands, feeling relaxed around his inmate. "City didn't have a lawman when you say you shot your brother, so no charges were filed back then. Why come forward now?"

Boone had his eyes shut. "I don't like getting played, sir."

"Mmm," Bass grunted. He'd already corresponded with Sheriff Clark in Fort Myers, asking about this Boone Larkin. The telegram he received back from the sheriff had read: EXEMPLARY CITIZEN, HARD WORKER. "Seems to me you doled out your own form of justice at the time . . . shootin' your leg and all."

"Mmm," Boone answered. He'd relayed to Bass the details of his self-inflicted wound, a failed attempt on the afternoon of the shooting to redirect the pain from his heart to his left calf.

Bass waited for any additional information, and when it didn't come, yanked up his dungarees and exited the cell area, his bootheels pounding a path along the wooden floorboards toward the sheriff's office.

• • •

An hour later, Boone listened to the sound of Bass preparing a second round of coffee. In the glow of a candle this morning, Boone had brewed his own pot at his parents' house. Awake before dawn, he'd understood—finally—that there was only one way to beat Tilly at her twisted game: admit to whatever she thought she had on him. Realizing what was required to become the one with leverage had taken him nearly a week, so what if he had to spend as much time or even more in jail? He figured the law was far less likely to deem him a murderer if he confessed to the accident before she could turn him in and imply worse. Ultimately, the truth would be revealed. He rubbed his neck and then sank his head as far as possible into the flat pillow. He'd have plenty of time to think in here—about Decker fuming, Belle's sweet face, and whether his parents would ever visit him in this place.

The place he hoped would free them all from the constraints of Tilly's damning lie.

• • •

Several days later, Boone awakened to the sound of something metal being raked across prison bars.

"Get outta bed," someone was commanding. Rubbing his eyes, Boone sat up on the cot.

"Your father's here." Marshal Bass stood outside the cell. "Sorry about this," he said, and held up an empty coffee mug. "Just don't get any prisoners of my own in here and I've always wanted to do that." He grinned.

"It was very impressive," Boone said, yawning and patting down his hair mussed from sleep.

A broad-shouldered man walked up, and Marshal Bass turned to him. "You can go in if you want, sir."

Sam Larkin offered the slightest nod, and Bass opened the cell with a long metal key. "Holler if you need anything," he said, presumably to his visitor.

"Oh, I will," Boone answered, prompting a smirk from Bass.

Boone's father took a seat on the empty cot parallel to the other bed. His tan skin was nearly as leathery as his belt, his build lean but muscular. He removed his straw hat and set it in his lap, its absence revealing a shock of wavy white hair. "What the hell are you doing in here, Son?"

Boone crossed his arms. "I'm forcing Tilly to tell the truth about Wyatt."

His father drew in a deep breath. "This stunt . . ." He shook his head. "Your mother and I stayed quiet to keep what you did a family matter. And now you've gone and ripped it all wide open, like a damn coyote gutting a calf."

Boone leaned forward, resting his elbows on his knees. "Pa, I haven't had my say here. I came home to repair things with you and Ma, and somehow I have a son?"

"Pesky, isn't it? Doesn't fit with your new life down south." He gripped his hat a little tighter.

"I did *not* bed Tilly, Pa. That boy belongs to some other cowboy," Boone said, his voice raised.

Suddenly, his father leaped up from the cot, dropped his hat, and lunged toward Boone, grabbing his shirt collar with both hands. The two wrestled on the cot as the older man unleashed a barrage of punches and as many harsh words.

"You shoot your brother square in the face, but you're not so good of a shot when the gun's aimed at you, huh?" His father was spitting mad. "Daniel's dead . . . and you. You only limp!"

Boone fought back with light jabs to his father's ribs but let the battle rage on.

"I'm sorry, Pa." He was breathing hard, speaking as best he could.

Boone wasn't bothered by the punches; in fact, he welcomed every blow. For years he'd wished his father had beaten him to a pulp after he'd shot Daniel. His immense shame would have welcomed severe physical pain, or any punishment at all. Instead, both parents had shut him out for the most part—though they had demanded he explain what happened that day: too much whiskey had led to a pretend gunfight in a hammock outside their cow camp.

Daniel had been ribbing Boone about not taking good care of his gun, practically begging Boone to give his *"dirty piece"* a try, to prove it even worked. Boone had attempted to count the bullets on the ground, but Daniel kept yapping, distracting him, daring him. His head had been swimming from whiskey and the tobacco from the cigar Daniel had given him. Finally, when Boone was sure he'd identified all six bullets in front of him, he'd pulled the trigger on his revolver.

Both parents had flinched when Boone described the moment he accidentally shot his brother in the face. None of them would ever forget the sight of Daniel's limp body draped across Judith, his head wrapped in a horse blanket. After Boone had finished explaining the tragic circumstances, it seemed to him that his parents did everything they could to erase the horrific images—and Boone himself—from their minds. From that point on, he had known that both he and his brother were ghosts.

"You slithered away like a snake, boy!" his father yelled, flipping Boone onto the cell floor.

Boone kept apologizing and his father kept yelling and swinging.

Marshal Bass appeared outside the cell, his trembling hand repeatedly missing the keyhole in the door. "No brawling! No brawling!" he yelled, finally inserting the key and turning it. Just as Boone's father landed a punch to his right eye, Marshal Bass belly flopped onto the men with a thud. Father and son both groaned, crushed by the lawman's bulk.

"That's enough!" Bass screamed, spread-eagle on the pile. He then rolled off and fumbled for a pair of handcuffs clipped to his belt. Seemingly unsure of which man to restrain, he said in a helpless tone, "I've only got one pair," and held out the dangling cuffs.

Between gulps of air, Boone's father said, "Don't bother. I'm leaving." He brushed himself off, grabbed his hat, and walked out of the cell.

Panting on the floor, Boone touched his mouth and checked his fingertips for blood. He was pleased to see that he had a busted lower lip.

Chapter 23

October was now in full swing, and the gut punch Belle had received from Boone still hurt deeply. Thank goodness that both the tomatoes and the clubs were flourishing, positive developments that helped offset her glum mood. Now, sitting in the cottage, she reread a letter that had arrived yesterday, its contents lifting everyone's spirits.

> *Dear Belle,*
>
> *All your hard work has paid off! The project update Fae and Mazie submitted has garnered enough support from the Florida chapter of home demonstration to launch your club into the state competition. Congratulations to all! The girls' battle with hornworms, aphids, and whitefly jumped right off the page. (Who knew pyrethrum powder could be portrayed as a hero?) Make sure the girls include at least one tomato recipe in their final booklets and write the club motto on the covers:* To make the best better.

I've enclosed information about accommodations in Sarasota as well as the requirements for the display booth and banner. I'm so proud of you! Keep up the good work and may the elements cooperate with your crop. Have Boone harrow the field several times in the weeks ahead.
Yours very sincerely,
Virginia

Belle smoothed a bent edge of Virginia's letter, thrilled that their experiment was working. The mention of Boone helping—and knowing he wouldn't—had upset her, but the fact that she'd made her friend proud was truly satisfying. She'd immediately written Virginia a response.

Dearest Virginia,
I cannot express how much joy your letter brings me and all of us! When I shared this development with both clubs, a cheer erupted the likes of which has not been heard since the Edisons lit up Seminole Lodge! Your news compels us to work even harder in the field and on our presentations.
I do have one concern. To be candid, Fae and Mazie are constantly wavering in their commitment to the club. I don't know if grief is an obstacle to their focus or if the rewards of self-confidence and community are just not compelling enough. I keep reminding those two that money or an elegant cut-glass bowl are on the line! Truly, they are sweet girls. Their imaginations are as robust as their frustrations . . . with each other, with the work, with what's been stolen from them. I must channel my

*inner Virginia and keep them moving forward.
(I'm imagining you smiling.)
    I will review the materials you send once I
receive them. In the meantime, we'll soon be on
the lookout for our first blooms.
    Your committed friend,
    Belle*

She gently rocked in the chair, pleased she'd shared her concerns about the girls with Virginia, whom she knew would understand. During their lunch weeks ago at Baker's, Virginia had explained that she'd once worked as a schoolteacher in her hometown. She'd described often feeling *like a cowhand wrangling her students' wandering minds*. That comment made even more sense now. Belle supposed that Fae and Mazie were no different from Virginia's students, with perhaps one exception: their pain likely transported them to particularly dark corners of the mind from time to time.

"Hold on," she said softly.

Belle got up from the chair and began to change clothes for tomato tending at Polk's. She would keep those two words in mind, for the girls and for herself.

• • •

Joseph Ritter hammered a bamboo pole into the ground next to a tomato plant. Both his hands were scarred from years of mishaps with whirling saw blades, but every finger was intact. The man's thick sideburns matched his brawny limbs and chest. "What kind of tomatoes have we got here?" he asked Fae and Mazie.

The sisters elbowed each other, as if to knock loose the answer. "Miss Belle?" Fae finally asked.

Belle handed Fae a watering can. "You know this. Think."

Fae passed the can to Mazie and stood with her hands on her hips. "Hmm . . . it starts with a *P*."

Paulette had an armful of bamboo and was handing Mr. Ritter stakes as they worked their way through the field. Hoping to minimize the distractions of family dynamics, the club had decided not to ask the girls' uncle to help in Boone's absence. And even though the business owner was busy working at his sawmill and filling in for Boone at the Lodge, he'd agreed to step in when asked. Duke had offered his help, too.

"Girls, the name of the tomatoes is featured in your song, for goodness' sake." Paulette began to sing, her voice a soothing soprano. "In our fertile one-tenth acre, blessed with sunshine by our maker, we keep watch from dusk to dawn, o'er our precious P—"

Both girls yelled, "Paragons!" Then they burst into laughter.

Mr. Ritter laughed, too. "Okay, so we're staking 'precious Paragons.'"

Fae flopped down to help the sawyer tie the lush plant to the stake. "Miss Belle says that staking helps the leaves catch the breeze, so they don't stay wet and rot."

Mr. Ritter glanced over at Belle, who was helping Mazie water. "Miss Belle and I are working together at the Edisons'. She's a very good gardener." He sat back on his scuffed bootheels. "Even the bees seem to listen to her."

Belle smiled at Mr. Ritter. She so appreciated his help while Boone was away. *Away rekindling his relationship with an old flame and bonding with his child.* The thought made her bang on the bottom of the upturned watering can, draining its last drop.

Whenever people asked when Boone was scheduled to return, she just shrugged and said there was no word yet. Last week, Merle had agreed to mail a box for her while he was in the town of Alva, where he planned to meet his honey vendor. He'd understood Belle's desire to avoid sending it from Fort

Myers, as Ida had a reputation for meddling with the mail. "I'll make sure Boone gets these cookies," Merle had assured her, unaware of the package's actual contents.

Belle looked out at the crop and drew in a breath of fresh autumn air. The tomatoes were growing and so was her nervous anticipation. The man who'd stolen, and then broken, her heart would soon receive his stashed letters—and a stinging message from her.

Chapter 24

Celia Larkin's anger with Boone had wrapped itself so tightly around her heart, it no longer felt like an organ; instead, it was more like a root-bound plant, trapped and stunted. Her youngest son had killed her oldest, then abandoned Wyatt and his mother. And after finally returning home, he'd had the gall to lie to all their faces. For weeks now, she'd stayed away from her son, too incensed to visit him in jail. Sam had been there once, but he'd allowed her to determine for herself what she wanted to do. She hadn't planned to go at all. But this morning, God had placed His hand on her heart, coaxing the knot of roots to loosen, to consider new growth. She hadn't been surprised. That was how God worked. Who was she to ignore His divine touch? And so, she was now standing in front of her son.

"What happened to your eye?" Celia asked, peering into Boone's cell.

"Pa and I had a fight a while back," Boone said, touching a small bruise near his right eye. "Almost healed."

The two of them were positioned on opposite sides of the steel bars. Celia had told Marshal Bass she wasn't staying long and didn't need to enter the cell.

"Your father didn't mention a fight," she said. "Never noticed a scratch on him."

"Well, I had it comin', Ma," Boone said softly. "You know that."

Celia took a small step backward and looked at her son. Handsome, strapping, seemingly vulnerable. He looked thinner. At that moment, the jagged hole in her soul seemed to cry out to him. *I've missed you. Please heal me.* If Boone would just admit the truth about Wyatt, they could be a family again.

"This came for you," she said, clutching a small box. "From Alva."

Boone crossed his arms. "Alva? Don't know anyone who lives there."

Celia tilted her head slightly. "Sure you don't have a girl there, too?"

"C'mon, Ma." Boone looked past her at the approaching marshal.

"I'll take that," Bass said, chewing something. "Gotta check everything that comes into the place." He took the package from her and headed back toward the office.

"Probably hoping there's food inside," Boone said with a slight grin.

Celia ignored the comment. "Son, you should know. Tilly and I have become quite close." She pulled her shawl tighter around her narrow shoulders. "After you left, no one would talk to me about . . . him."

"Daniel, Ma." Boone spoke gently.

"Daniel . . . ," she said, her throat catching. She reached up and rubbed the small silver cross hanging around her neck. "Daniel was everywhere in our house. His boots, those little wooden chickens he whittled for me, the banged-up canteen he used on every ride."

She looked past Boone. "I don't know if your father talked to anybody about Daniel. Maybe he talked to the cows or to the moon about that horrible day. I don't know. But he didn't talk to me about him. In fact, he made it clear that Daniel's name wasn't to be spoken anymore." Tears welled up in her eyes and she let go of the cross. "He didn't want to talk about Daniel, but I did. My son deserved to be remembered . . . out loud." She paused to dab her eyes with the hem of her shawl. "When Tilly started coming around, she let me talk. She listened."

Boone said softly, "Tilly's not who you think she is, Ma."

"Stop. Just *stop*, Boone." Her tone was firm, not harsh. "She's my grandson's mother," she insisted. "This little boy was an answer to my prayers for something, anything, to lessen the pain. Don't you see? He gave us new life and hope for a brighter future." She searched Boone's face. "You're his father, honey, and he's a blessing to us all. Surely you understand. Wyatt is the bright light we need." Her voice cracked. "There's been so much darkness." Tears were streaming down her face.

Boone reached through the cell bars and offered her his hands. She took them, her shoulders shaking as she wept. "He's a beautiful little boy, Ma."

Celia cried even harder. She loved her sons so dearly. Boone should love his, too. "God tells us to forgive, Boone," she said through sobs. "I forgive you, but please . . . just . . ."

"We're going to be all right, Ma," Boone said, squeezing her hands.

Oh, how she desperately wanted to trust him, to believe his words. But if Boone could look into the sweet face of his own son and lie, how could any of them ever be *all right*?

• • •

Having been locked up for weeks now, Boone was getting used to the daily scents and sounds produced by Bass filling in for the sheriff. The marshal fixed coffee in the morning and the afternoon. His hands frequently rifled through a desk drawer for who knows what. His boots struck the floor as if they had boulders—not feet—inside of them.

Now, half an hour after his ma's departure, those heavy heels were pounding his way. Boone stood up from the cot just as the marshal stopped outside his cell.

"Just a box full of letters," Bass said, shoving a stack of envelopes through the chow hole in the bars.

Boone grabbed them. "Anything else in the box, or did you already eat it?"

"Guess you'll never know," Bass said, palming his holster as he sauntered away.

The yellow silk ribbon wrapped around the letters was tied haphazardly, probably the handiwork of Bass's fat fingers. Had the lawman read through the letters? Boone didn't care. After all, he didn't recognize the small bundle.

Sitting on his cot, he opened the top envelope and pulled out the letter. As he began to read, the message confused him. The writing was racy, and the note was signed, "Yours, T." He pulled out the next letter and read it, too, the words again directed at "Roo." As he continued to read and absorb the specific details, Boone's heart sank. A shocking scenario was unfolding before his eyes. By the time he finished reading the last letter, he had to work mightily to resist the urge to rip up every one of them.

But Boone knew the notes had to stay intact. They were the very evidence he needed to finally move on from his past, to resolve his present, and to secure the future he'd long dreamed of—with Belle.

Chapter 25

Just when the flawless November weather couldn't get any better, the tomato crop took an unexpected turn for the worse. More than a week earlier, the vibrant plants had delighted the women and girls with their tiny yellow blooms. Abigail had even thrown a special lunch in Baker's backyard, complete with table bouquets provided by Belle. The girls had brought their booklets and sketched drawings that featured five petals and a stamen, renderings of the dainty flowers that would soon turn into tomatoes.

But since that lunch, the plants hadn't progressed. They were mature and hugging the stakes, but even after a hearty harrow by Merle and consistent watering by the girls, they were fading.

Belle and Alice stood in the field, assessing the damage.

"The leaves are turning yellow, the whole thing is wilting, and it's not getting water to make food," Belle said, crouching next to a limp tomato plant.

Alice heaved a sigh. "Coconut peed on a few of the plants," she admitted. "We're very sorry."

Belle forced a smile. "Coconut's in the clear, Alice. A dog couldn't cause all of this."

Yesterday, others in the Circle Club had walked the acreage, too. Poppy had even said a prayer over the field in hopes of some sort of resurrection. Behind closed doors, the women had discussed whether the girls, tired of the project, could have sabotaged the crop. Quickly, though, they'd dismissed that theory, each of them sharing examples of how Fae and Mazie had seemed excited about both the future harvest and the prospect of canning. Ultimately, they'd decided that the trip to Sarasota for the state competition should be canceled.

"I suppose I need to head over to talk to the Dawsons," Belle said as she stood back up.

"Want some company?" Alice asked.

"No, thanks," Belle said. "I don't think even you could make sharing this news with the girls any easier."

The two friends left the tomato field, then Belle walked alone to Clay's shop, where she knew the sisters were working on a club project.

• • •

When Belle entered Dawson's cabinet shop, Clay, Edwina, and the girls were painting a banner for the club's booth.

"Look, Miss Belle!" Fae said, dotting the *i* in "Girls'" with red paint. Mazie was beaming, too, and announced, "Lee County Girls' Tomato Club. That's us!" She bent down, scooped up a handful of sawdust, and tossed it into the air like confetti.

Belle made herself smile and toss confetti, too. It seemed unnecessary to tamp the group's enthusiasm right then. She'd have to be honest with the Dawsons soon enough, but for now she allowed them to continue with their fun, said goodbye, and headed down Front Street toward the Western Union office.

• • •

Oscar Powell was well regarded in town. Not only was he a decent man, he also expertly managed the urgent communications that regularly zinged in and out of Fort Myers over the telegraph lines. The fact that he was friends with Mr. Edison was yet another reason folks admired him.

"Why, hello there, Belle," Oscar said when she walked in. As usual, his clothes reflected the importance of his job—shirtsleeves with decorative studs, black ribbon tie, ironed trousers, and shiny shoes. It was a well-known fact that his wife, Jeannie, kept her husband's wardrobe well cuffed and buffed.

"Hello, Mr. Powell," Belle said. "I hope I'm not interrupting."

"Not at all," he said, waving her into the room. "Have a seat."

The chair he pointed to was covered in papers, so she grabbed the pile and held it up. "Over here all right?" she asked, nodding toward a table covered in even more paper.

"Oh, sure. I have it all filed right up here," Oscar said, thumping his temple.

Belle set down the stack and took a seat. "I need to send a telegram to Tennessee."

Oscar grinned and began tapping the knob on his telegraph key. "Dear Tennessee . . ." He winked at her.

"Oh, of course," Belle said, and pulled out a sheet of paper from her pocket. After she'd named the telegraph station closest to where Virginia lived, he indicated he was ready.

Belle cleared her throat. "Virginia, bad news from the tomato patch. Crop has died. No answers and . . ."

Then she stopped talking, surprised by the thick lump in her throat. Suddenly, failure in the garden and heartbreak over Boone joined forces, overwhelming her at this very inopportune time. Tears began to well up in her eyes, and her brows furrowed. *Oh no.* If she could have buried herself under Oscar's mounds of paperwork, she would have.

"Miss Belle?" Oscar lowered his spectacles and took a good look at her. When he saw tears rolling down her cheeks, he yelled, "Jeannie!"

Mrs. Powell appeared immediately from a back room, gripping the handle of a flat iron. "What is it, dear?"

Oscar pointed at Belle, who was attempting unsuccessfully to dry her runny nose even as she wept. He kept jabbing the air, pointing, his eyes panicked.

Without hesitation, Jeannie sprang into action. She set down the hot iron in a metal tray on Oscar's desk, then plucked a handkerchief from his breast pocket as she scurried past him.

"Here you go, honey," she said, handing over the hankie.

Belle took it and started talking into it, her words barely understandable through the sobbing and sniffling.

". . . all died . . . button ring . . ."

When she stopped breathing, paralyzed with sorrow, Oscar frantically tapped his telegraph key over and over. The hammering roused her, and Belle blew her nose into the hankie. She continued to mumble.

"That ridiculous nickname . . . cows and creeks and . . ." She was making no sense, but neither the telegraph operator nor his wife attempted to understand.

When she finally fell silent and settled, Belle drew in a deep breath and then exhaled. "I am so embarrassed, Mr. and Mrs. Powell." She dabbed her eyes.

"Don't be silly," Jeannie said. Without missing a beat, she added, "Oscar, read me back the telegram."

Oscar did as he was told. "'Virginia, bad news from the tomato patch. Crop has died. No answers and.'" He glanced at Belle, as if checking to see whether the waterworks had resumed.

Jeannie pulled up a chair next to Belle and sat down on the papers spread across its seat. "What has you so upset, dear?"

Belle twisted the handkerchief as she spoke and considered

her words carefully. "I suppose I feel like a failure. The tomatoes we were growing all died, and now the girls I've been teaching don't have anything to can for the state competition. We're allowed to compete without them, but I don't think I should put the girls through that."

Jeannie's face lit up. "Well, I've got tomatoes, honey. So does Mrs. Hadley and Mrs. Abbott, and lots of women in town. The girls can have ours."

"Oh, goodness," Belle said. She slid forward on her seat and put her hand on Mrs. Powell's knee. "That's so very kind of you, thank you, but . . ."

Then she paused. *But what?* She began to imagine Eva sitting across from her, holding her hands, guiding her with a mother's love. She then considered the girls' aunt, Edwina, and the club members. They were mothering Fae and Mazie, just as she was. Surely, the strong women who'd lifted her up— Abigail and Grace Bailey—were with her right now. Belle sat up straighter. Gutsy Virginia was nearby, too.

"Actually, I think it's best the girls learn that life doesn't always go a person's way." She nodded as she spoke. "And that no matter what, you show up and do your best." Her voice was strong. "I'm a firm believer in . . . well, in digging deep."

She turned toward Oscar, who flashed an enormous smile, obviously uncomfortable. "Let's begin again, please, Mr. Powell." Belle cleared her throat. "Virginia, we are coming to Sarasota without tomatoes, to make the best better."

As Mr. Powell tapped out a series of dots and dashes, the spirited rhythm seemed to clear the room of any previous unease. The atmosphere was now as festive as a flurry of sawdust confetti.

Jeannie looked over at Belle and smiled. "Atta girl," she said.

Chapter 26

Yesterday, Boone had asked Marshal Bass to summon his parents to the jail for a visit. He hadn't been sure they would come. But now his mother and father were sitting across from him on the other cot.

"I have some news," Boone said, looking down at a pile of papers in his lap. "I received these letters in the mail."

"Were they in the box from Alva?" his mother asked. She was sitting close to her husband, a Bible placed next to her on the bed.

"Yes, Ma. I don't know why they came from there." Boone was still staring at the letters.

His father cleared his throat. "You asked us here. What do you want?"

Boone looked up. For a moment, he just stared at his parents. For hours, he'd wavered about what to do. He now had proof concerning the identity of Wyatt's father, but revealing those facts could seem selfish and even cruel. As he sat alone in the cell, competing feelings had engaged in a heated grappling match. At first, a deep desire for Redemption had put Guilt in a choke hold. But then Guilt had performed a slick move and pinned Redemption to the ground. On and on the sparring had continued as Boone tried to decide just what to reveal to his parents.

"Pa, what I want is for this never to have happened to our family," Boone said softly. "None of it."

His father crossed his arms. "Well, it didn't just *happen*, Boone," he said. "You caused it. All of it."

Celia turned toward her husband. "Sam . . . ," she said. "Let's just listen to him."

"Why? He's not saying much of anything," Sam insisted, his voice raised.

"Boone," his mother said, "if you would just stop lying to us. We know you were sweet on Tilly." Nearly begging, she added, "Please, Son."

Boone looked at his mother's aging face, the creases around her eyes no doubt deeper for all the tears she'd cried over what he'd done to Daniel. Her Bible was tucked next to her, as was so often the case, her small hands clasped in her lap. How many times in recent years had she held them just like that, praying for Daniel . . . and maybe even for him? He was deeply grateful for the loving gift of forgiveness she'd granted as they faced one another through the metal bars. His mother had revealed herself to be a remarkable woman, somehow finding the strength to offer him mercy. Now she was asking something of him.

Please, Son.

Right then and there, he decided it was best to grant his mother's heartfelt wish: that he simply tell the truth.

"Okay then, Ma," Boone said, his voice cracking. Slowly, he handed the stack in his lap over to his mother, who took it, her eyes locked on Boone.

With a loud sigh, she unfolded a letter and began to read. When she finished that one, she opened another. And another. Finally, she whispered, "Oh, dear."

"What is it . . . ?" His father grabbed a letter for himself. His face didn't change at first, but then his eyes widened as he read two, then three. Boone sat watching as Saint Daniel was revealed to be just another flawed soul.

After a long silence, his father spoke. "So, that's your story?" The paper in his hand crinkled from his tightening grip. "That's the reason you shot your brother?"

"No, Pa. I had no idea," Boone said. He added softly, "And I hope to God that's not what Daniel somehow thought as he passed."

"But your brother would *never* do this to you," his mother insisted softly.

Boone shrugged. "The letters prove he did, Ma." He shook his head. "I didn't want to believe it either, but as you can see with your own eyes, Tilly—or "T"—was writing to Daniel. We all know who Roo is."

And they all did. From the time he was little, Daniel's nickname had been Roo. As a boy, he'd been so at ease on a horse that his father had dubbed him their little "buckaroo." Soon, the moniker was shortened to Roo, and then, over the years, was used interchangeably with Daniel's actual name by the people closest to him, though never by fellow cow hunters.

"Ma?" Boone asked. His mother now knew that he'd not only killed Daniel but also her grandson's father. "Can you still forgive me?"

Celia shut her eyes and sighed. As she reopened them, she laid her hand on the Bible and said, "Yes, Son. I have no say in the matter."

Boone's father set the last letter aside and rubbed his scruffy chin. He then got up and walked back and forth in the cell for a moment. Finally, he said, "So you're saying that Wyatt is Daniel's boy?"

Boone pointed toward the other cot. "Those letters are saying it, Pa. Wyatt may look like me, but I look like Daniel."

He picked up the yellow ribbon off the cot and laid it across his knee. "Look, I didn't even realize I had these letters."

When his father sat back down, Boone explained that the woman he was in love with, Belle, had placed a note on top of the letters, saying she'd found them in a sack under his bed while tidying up his boat. After racking his brain, he'd recalled grabbing a few of Daniel's belongings before leaving Kissimmee. Still in a fog, he'd bagged items like his brother's bandannas and a belt. He'd also taken a box he'd assumed held Daniel's cigars, but instead Tilly's letters were tucked inside.

"I just wanted to take some of him with me," Boone said, looking down at the ribbon. "And then the sack stayed out of sight on my boat. Or maybe I couldn't get myself to go through it." He shook his head. When he looked up, he saw that his mother's bottom lip was quivering.

"I understand. I still hang Daniel's shirts on the line from time to time," she said. "And I bake his favorite cookies." She pulled out a handkerchief from her skirt pocket and dabbed at her eyes.

Boone was surprised to see his father reach over and take his mother's hand. Maybe mother and son weren't the only ones who were finally ready to reconcile.

"These letters," Sam said. "Why did they arrive in a package from Alva, Son?"

"I'm not sure, Pa. You say the letter I mailed to you from Fort Myers never arrived, so maybe Belle was trying to avoid some shady business at the local post office. It's been a problem."

"Hmm . . . ," Sam replied.

Boone could tell his father was still trying to process the shocking news and judge its validity. His thoughts then shifted to Belle. She must have used the return address on the letter he'd sent her from Kissimmee. He could only imagine how deeply devastated she was by the discovery. She'd already been brutalized by one man, and now—seemingly—deceived by another, the one she'd trusted with her past, present, and future. "Your secret is out," she'd scribbled on a note inside the box. If her words could've reached up and choked him, they would have. What a devastating misunderstanding. Knowing Belle as he did, he doubted she'd been willing to talk to anyone about this. If that was true, she now thought she was harboring yet another dreadful secret. He had to get back to her.

"But the letter we got from Fort Myers called your girl an 'unruly filly,'" his mother said. "Claimed she's stirring up trouble in town."

Damn Ida . . . , Boone thought. "Ma, Belle is nothing like any of that nonsense." He recalled "his girl" jumping up and down, announcing their engagement to the tomato plants. "She's kind and strong. And far from unruly. The person who wrote that letter is a liar." He added softly, "There's been enough lying."

No one spoke for a few minutes. Inside the musty cell, the family sat in silence, waiting for sorrow, anger, and ideally grace to weigh in on all that had been revealed about Daniel, and about what had happened in the past.

• • •

Daniel was lying on a patchwork quilt, legs crossed, leaning against his bed's slatted cypress backboard. The door to his room was closed, even though he knew his parents and Boone were in town stocking up on provisions. He'd agreed to stay behind and weed his mother's gardens, to him a project more tolerable than shopping, but still quite time-consuming. The backyard garden was a handful, a 400-square-foot cluster of vegetables plus a border of flowers his mother called her *bait for pollinators*. He tried his best to remove only invaders when he weeded, but once he'd pulled up all her early carrots and caught hell for a month. Her herb garden, planted in an old canoe in the front yard, was more pleasant to tend. As he yanked out dandelions or crabgrass, the aroma of mint and lavender would waft through the air. He even enjoyed chewing on basil leaves as he worked.

Now, though, on this hazy Saturday afternoon, his chores were complete and he was relaxing in his bedroom, boots off.

He was eager to open the envelope he'd plucked from the crisscross boots of a cabbage palm growing down the road from the Larkin home, just as he and the letter writer had arranged. As he looked down at the paper beside him, he untied a sweaty, frayed bandanna from around his neck and laid it out on the bed to dry. Then he picked up the envelope, held it under his nose, and took a long whiff. It didn't smell as strong as some of the other notes, but he thought he could detect a hint of Tilly's perfume. Using his thumb, he tore open the envelope and pulled out the letter. As all the others had been, the note inside was brief.

> *To my Roo—*
> *I can't stop thinking about our time in the*
> *loft. Do you think we kept the cows up?*
> *Yours, T*

Daniel grinned at the little hearts Tilly used to dot her *i*'s. She even did that when she was drawing words out on his skin, like *Kiss me now*. The girl was an intoxicating mix of femininity and forthrightness. Hearts and haylofts. She was the one who'd led him up the ladder in her family's dairy barn and ravaged him in the loft, and he'd certainly let her. Daniel reread her question. Yes, they'd clearly kept the cows awake. There had been as much mooing as there'd been moaning inside the Browns' barn that evening.

The two of them had met through Boone. One day, his

brother had been riding by the Tropical Hotel after picking up fabric for their mother at Makinson & Katz downtown. As Boone and Tilly told the story, she'd simply been taking a break from cleaning rooms when she became *overly engaged* by a man who said he worked in a turpentine camp. Boone had noticed her outstretched arm against the man's chest, dismounted, and pretended to be Tilly's boyfriend, a ploy that successfully disengaged the man. After that, Tilly and Boone had struck up a friendship. The pair would sometimes take a stroll along Lake Tohopekaliga after she'd left work, or she'd bring her horse to the Larkins'—the Browns lived nearby—and the two would take a long ride. Because he and Boone were close, Daniel knew that his brother had kissed Tilly a number of times and thought she was sweet.

"Oh, I am one god-awful brother," Daniel said quietly, leaning his head against the backboard.

Yes. Tilly *was* sweet, but she was sneaky, too. She'd turned him into a person he didn't recognize . . . or respect. She kept tempting him and he kept touching her. Just the other day he'd been cooling off in the Little Buck, a wide but shallow creek that ran along undeveloped property not far from his family's house. Boone had been at the livery washing Judith when Daniel had decided to take a dip. Somehow, Tilly had known he was there and showed up while he was floating in place.

"We can't keep doing this, Tilly," he'd said to her.

"Doing what?" the girl had asked, and proceeded to strip down, revealing her plain undergarments and eye-catching curves, now so familiar to him. The sight of her naked body had aroused him yet again. He knew what she'd feel like before she even took a step into the water.

That creek, the loft, the everywhere of it all disgusted Daniel. How could he repeatedly betray his brother? Or do so even once? He'd convinced himself that Boone and Tilly didn't really mean anything to each other. But did they? Boone had never told Daniel he was falling for Tilly. In fact, he'd said he hadn't slept with her, and based on what Daniel had experienced with Tilly—uninhibited, aggressive Tilly—he was certain his brother had been offered many opportunities. Daniel wasn't sure if he was falling for her himself. He loved the way she made him feel, but only for about twenty minutes. After that, he felt guilty and scummy and not like the man he wanted to be. He knew he should tell Boone, but it almost felt too late now; he'd clearly fractured their brotherly bond. Or maybe Boone would forgive him if he confessed. Boone was like their ma—gentle and understanding.

"Dammit," he cussed, and shoved the letter back into the envelope. This entire self-inflicted situation was so confounding.

Daniel got up off the bed and walked over to his bureau. After pulling open the top drawer, he grabbed a cigar box inside and set it atop the dresser. He opened the lid and looked down at a small stack of envelopes inside the box. He untied Tilly's yellow silk hair ribbon and added her latest letter to the others. Then he retied the ribbon, closed the lid, and cursed himself for bedding Tilly and betraying Boone.

• • •

Inside the cell, the Larkins had been silent for a while. Finally, Celia spoke.

"I wonder if Daniel wanted you to shoot him, Boone?" she asked, staring straight ahead.

"For the love of . . . ," his father muttered.

Celia interrupted. "Sam, I remember Boone telling us that Daniel dared him to pull the trigger," she said. "And please, watch your language."

"Dammit, Celia, that's what brothers do," Sam said,

ignoring her request. "They test each other," he insisted, but he glanced over at Boone.

Boone squinted at his mother, stunned by her theory. He considered it. Had his brother been goading him that day? Daring him to fire his gun? The fake gunfight *had* been Daniel's idea. And the drinking and smoking, too. Boone had sensed the combination was ill-advised but trusted his big brother. Plus, the booze had blurred his judgment right along with his vision. *One, two, three . . .* He recalled trying to count the bullets he'd removed from each chamber, but Daniel kept yelling, "Just shoot that clunker, baby brother!" Had Daniel assumed that if he did, Boone would merely graze him? Scar him as payment for what he'd done with Tilly? Had Daniel planned to ever tell the family about her pregnancy? Boone sighed and looked up at the ceiling, frustrated. He knew the answers to his nagging questions would forever haunt and elude him.

"Marshal!" his father suddenly yelled, startling the others.

Boone looked at him. Had his father accepted the truth about Tilly and Daniel? Could their family "messes" be redefined? They were, after all, just imperfect people slogging their way through life.

Bass appeared, tucking in his shirttails. The man was always on the verge of appearing professional.

"We need to get out of this jail," his father said firmly.

"Yup," Bass said, rooting around in his pocket for the key.

When the door rattled open, his parents headed for the exit. As they moved past Bass, Boone's father looked back at him. "We're *all* getting out," he announced.

Boone didn't waste a second. He stood up, grabbed his hat, and walked out of the cell.

"Give my regards to Sheriff Clark," Bass said to Boone. "He says you're working hard down there."

Boone stuck out his hand and Bass took it. "Just working on some fences, sir."

The time had finally come for Boone to go home, and to see what freedom might look like for him and his family.

Chapter 27

Belle admired her nicest outfit, a striped Empire-cut dress she'd draped across her bed. The squared neckline and short gathered sleeves were a welcome change from her everyday clothes. She looked in the mirror and gathered her loose hair, thick like a horse's mane. Maybe she'd wear it down for the contest, but for now she wove it into a side braid. Perhaps at this same moment, Edwina and Clay were helping the girls pack, too, as they'd be leaving for Sarasota in a few days. Belle was pleased with her decision to keep news of the experimental club's participation in the competition out of the *Press*. The girls didn't need any added pressure to perform.

When Belle told them the trip was still on despite the lost crop, she'd given them her best speech about *showing up* and *seeing things through*. They were forging ahead to the state competition to represent Lee County, heads held high. To her surprise, Fae and Mazie had risen to the occasion, writing passages in their booklets that had brought tears to her eyes.

Fae's read:

Miss Belle once told us that blood is thicker than water. We didn't understand and may not still, but I think it means that us sisters need to stick together. Growing tomatoes has brought Mazie and me closer, especially when our crop died. We went through dying together already, so losing plants isn't so bad. We can grow them again next year.

And Mazie had written:

My sister and me didn't know how much the folks in our town were looking out for us. Many neighbors offered up their tomatoes when they learned ours died. Fae and I thought Uncle Clay and Aunt Edwina were the only ones who loved us, but now we know different. Family is all around us.

Belle knew that Virginia would be very proud when she read through the girls' booklets. As she began to brush off a pair of calfskin boots, someone knocked on her cottage door. When Belle opened it, Jeannie Powell was standing on her front porch, waving a small piece of paper back and forth.

"I wanted to hand deliver this myself, Belle." She smiled. "I just *knew* it was more than tomatoes that was bothering you."

Belle moved back from the door. "Please, Mrs. Powell, come in."

She sat down on her bed and stroked Coquina, while Jeannie took a seat in a rocking chair near the gateleg table.

"I'm never nosy about telegrams that come in, but Oscar himself scooted this one my way." She handed it to Belle. "Take a look."

Silently, Belle began to read the brief message.

BELLE GOOD NEWS

Just then, there came another knock on the door; Belle didn't want to stop reading but got up and pulled it open.

"Merle?" she said, surprised to see him during work hours.

"Can I come in, honey?" he asked.

"Of course," Belle said, and led him inside. "Mrs. Powell's here."

Merle looked surprised. "Everything okay, Jeannie?"

"Oh, sure," she said. The cat was now curled up in her lap.

All Belle wanted to do was read the telegram, but she stayed put next to Merle. The three just looked at each other.

"Well, I guess I'll go first," Merle said. "Sheriff Clark stopped by Duggan's a bit ago."

Belle touched Merle's arm. "Everything all right?"

"Well, Sheriff said the marshal in Kissimmee alerted him that Boone was in jail over there, but no charges were filed and now he's . . ."

Jeannie interrupted Merle, swatting at the air. "Oh, I'm not worried about that," she said, and scratched Coquina on the head.

"Why is Boone in jail?" Belle asked, moving toward the bed. She grabbed the telegram and read it in full.

BELLE GOOD NEWS OUT OF JAIL ROO IS
DANIEL I HAVE A NEPHEW MA IS HAPPY
PA AND I ARE TALKING COWS AGAIN
CAN'T WAIT TO SEE YOU MY LOVE

Belle looked up at Jeannie, wide-eyed. "Roo is Daniel!"

Jeannie smiled. "I have no idea what that means, but I do know this telegram proves you didn't fail at anything, honey. He loves you."

"Oh, Jeannie!" Belle cried, going to her and kissing her

cheek. Relieved and excited, she yanked open a side drawer on the table and grabbed a pencil. "Would you please dictate a telegram to Mr. Powell for me when you get home?"

Merle scratched his head. "Who's Roo?"

Belle held up a *wait a minute* finger toward Merle and sat down on the bed. She began to speak and write the words for her telegram at the same time. "'Meet us in three days.'" She scribbled more and identified the hotel: "'The DeSoto in Sarasota.'" She then wrote down Boone's address for locating the nearest telegraph station and added, "Oh . . . and 'love, Belle!'"

Jeannie gently launched the cat from her lap and took the telegram. "Happy to do it, Belle." She asked Merle, "Walk me back?"

Merle looked at Belle.

"Go on," Belle said. "I promise it will all make sense soon."

He shrugged. "If you're happy, I'm happy, honey." He held his arm out to Jeannie. "But I do expect some details from you, ma'am."

Jeannie smiled and looped her arm through his. "Like Oscar says, 'Let's dot, dot, and dash,'" she said, and the pair left, laughing.

Chapter 28

Boone had spent nearly two months in Kissimmee, the bulk of it thirty feet from Marshal Bass and the last few days with his family. Though he had wanted more than anything to return to Belle, he knew it was important to reestablish a sound foundation before leaving his parents' home this time. Their interactions had been of the simple kind—sharing meals, tackling home repairs, catching up on where the cows were grazing—and each one had been pleasant. He'd played with Wyatt often, and when he'd offered to build a roping dummy for him, the youngster had performed a little jig, which had made everyone laugh. The eager boy had helped him with the task, handing Boone nails as he hammered together boards until a calflike creature took shape. When Wyatt asked what he was going to use for its *antlers*, Boone explained that their little dogie wasn't old enough yet for horns.

While they worked, Tilly remained in the house talking with Celia, giving Boone space to interact with his nephew. The adults had agreed that whatever unease remained after such jarring events, the little boy's well-being should be everyone's priority. To no one's surprise, Wyatt quickly caught on to coiling a rope and generating the action needed to launch the lasso in range of the calf. The young buckaroo managed to hit his target within an hour of training.

"I done it, Uncle Boone!" he'd declared, racing to the calf to confirm his catch.

Just recently, the Larkins and Tilly had told the child that, sadly, his father—whom Wyatt had not met and thought was on an extended cattle drive—was killed by a rustler along the trail. Wyatt had cried but didn't take long to return to his loving, curious little self. Now the boy seemed intrigued and delighted with his newly met uncle, and he'd tagged alongside Boone as often as possible, peppering him with questions about his father's favorite horse and whether his pa had loved roasted chicken as much as he did. For Boone, talking to Wyatt about Daniel had been comforting and enjoyable. He hoped the rest of the family had found their own conversations about Daniel restorative, too.

On this, his last day, Boone was scheduled to take an evening train, so his mother had packed food for him to eat in the railcar. After saying his goodbyes and receiving hugs from everyone—including an awkward embrace from a newly humbled Tilly—Boone had begun his walk to the train depot. His visit home had been a little bit of everything—challenging, revealing, rewarding. And it wasn't quite over yet. Now, as the sun melted into the horizon, Boone turned where instructed, using directions written on a slip of paper he'd pulled from his pocket.

When Boone arrived at his destination, fireflies were flashing secret codes. Crickets chirped incessantly, and the evening air felt close around him. Or maybe he was just sticky from nerves. As he walked through the Rose Hill Cemetery, there was still enough light to guide him to where he needed to go. He'd grabbed a used candle from a pile at the graveyard entrance for his eventual exit in the dark. Following the diagram his mother had drawn for him, Boone wandered among the headstones until he found what he was looking for.

"Howdy, Brother," he said softly, and looked down at the simple grave marker. He glanced at the dates etched in the sandstone, then turned away and sat on the ground. He couldn't bear to stare at such stark and finite figures. Boone's parents had told him they'd recently bought a proper stone for their son but had left off the Larkin name to be discreet. Even though Daniel was buried at home in a secluded area of their property, his mother had insisted last year that her boy be represented in a proper place where the dead are revered. Boone thought the purchase illogical, but who was he to question a mother's search for even an ounce of comfort? And in any case, he was more than fine with that decision; he didn't want to visit his brother in the backyard or be reminded of having buried him there. Besides, Daniel wasn't really in the yard or the cemetery. He was with God.

"We had a laugh yesterday, remembering your trouble with the carrots, so I brought you some," Boone said. He reached into his pack and pulled out a small bunch, the vegetables' once-feathery tops now wilted. "Pa just about had a come apart when he found out what you did to Ma's crop." Boone smiled and shook his head. "Pa always hated to see her disappointed, didn't he?"

Boone's trip to the cemetery had been a last-minute decision. Rather, his mother had decided for him when she'd requested he go. She never asked for much, and of course it made sense that he see the marker while in town. Maybe it was why that old song had popped into his head. *Do not let your chances, like sunbeams pass you by, for you never miss the water till the well runs dry.*

Still, Boone had dreaded visiting the cemetery on the way over. The reality of whose gravestone was there, and the unnatural order of it all, had tied his stomach in knots. He'd thought the carrots might help start a "conversation" but knew that the one-sided nature of it would be awkward. And it was. If only he and his brother were arguing over who got the mosquito net at cow camp. Or joshing each other about who chopped wood the fastest. But they weren't.

"Look, Daniel . . ."

Instantly, Boone's throat locked up. His lower lip began to quiver, and he had to force the words out.

"You've got a son, Brother." The five words hit him with the power of the train waiting for him. Guilt, pain, and sadness leveled him, and he began to cry. "I'm so sorry, Daniel," he whispered. His broad shoulders shook as he sobbed. He covered his face with his hands, but they were trembling so much he let them drop to the ground.

He dug his fingers into the sandy soil, squeezing it in frustration. If only Daniel could be there with him. As brothers, as friends, they could work through all that had happened, all that had been revealed. They could share how much they meant to each other. But now they never would. The inability to do any of these things was for him one of the most anguishing aspects of Daniel's death, a fact made even worse by the knowledge that he was the one who'd caused it.

"I love you, Daniel," he whispered through sobs.

Boone wept until he'd cried himself out, the release exhausting but necessary, and inevitable. He used his sleeves to wipe his face and took deep breaths to calm himself. The cemetery had grown dark, and he needed to head for the nearby depot. He fumbled around his pack for matches and then lit the black wick of the stubby candle. He moved the carrots to the foot of the headstone and used it to stand up. With a hand atop the grave marker, he said softly, "I'll get to know Wyatt, and when I see you again, we'll saddle up and I'll tell you all about him." He gently patted the stone. "So long for now, Brother."

He turned away from the gravestone and began to walk through the cemetery by candlelight. When he heard the train whistle, he picked up his pace. He promised himself that the next time he communicated with his parents, he'd suggest they add the name Larkin to Daniel's marker. The family had nothing to hide anymore.

Especially not the way they felt about each other.

Chapter 29

Historically, Sarasota had been recognized for its fishing industry, but two years ago the town landed its first luxury hotel, the DeSoto, its newest claim to fame. Using lumber shipped in from Cedar Key and Apalachicola, crews had built an impressive structure that rose three stories and was crowned with an observation tower boasting windows on each side. An American flag waved above it all. With thirty rooms, a sprawling lobby, and fine dining, the hotel was touted as "a place for those of wealth and influence." For the next two days, though, the DeSoto would also be a place for those with a different kind of wealth: that of knowledge and of countless crates of canned tomatoes.

"No riding on it," Belle admonished Mazie. The girl was trying to hop aboard the bellman's cart, stacked with their luggage and the rolled-up Lee County banner. The hotel lobby was busier than the street outside, jammed with carts that were rolling dangerously close to each other. All around, clusters of tomato girls chitchatted and explored the elegant surroundings. Some well-heeled guests prodded their valets like racehorses, trying desperately to escape the din generated by the excited young girls. The hotel's double-decker verandas were milling with people, too, drawn there by sunny skies and flowery words printed in the hotel brochure: "Charming views of the bayfront and a brilliant pageant of carriages on Main Street all day long." While the DeSoto charged high rates for its luxe amenities, guests on the porches knew November's warmth and gentle breeze were free of charge.

Belle and the girls arrived in Sarasota tired, having taken a schooner downriver, then a steamboat north. Although Manatee County was small—population 2,800—it was still twice the size of Lee County. The promise of new and exciting experiences helped to energize the trio.

"When will we see Miss Virginia?" Mazie asked, rubbing her eyes and spinning like a ballerina.

With one hand on the cart, Belle looked around as they waited in line to check in. "Soon, I hope." Virginia's presence would surely calm her nerves. Wrangling the girls and anticipating the competition had left her a bit rattled.

As if Virginia had read her thoughts, the stocky woman suddenly cut through the throng like a tugboat, smiling and excusing herself as she politely but confidently carved her way toward the Lee County contingent.

"Now here's my favorite club!" she said, and hugged the group, her solid frame roomy enough for all three bodies to fit within her arms.

When they parted, Belle said, "Oh, I'm so very glad to see you, Virginia."

"Me too!" the sisters both declared.

"It's a beautiful hotel," Belle said, dragging the cart a few feet forward.

"With such beautiful people," Fae added. She was staring at a woman at the front of the line who was wearing an otter-pelt coat, her cart stacked with shiny leather suitcases and round hat boxes.

Virginia leaned sideways to see what Fae was talking about. "Oh, she's just showing off, honey. It's hardly fur weather, for heaven's sake." She knelt down next to the girls. "See the ratty way she's speaking to the desk clerk? Nice clothes don't always mean there's nice people underneath them."

Belle couldn't help herself. "Like Mrs. Cravin."

Virginia stood and pulled a small notebook from her dress pocket and reviewed it. "After you check in, get settled and take a nap, or do whatever you have to do to think straight." She eyed the cart. "I see you have your banner. You'll be supplied with a table tomorrow." She pointed two fingers at the girls. "Booklets?" Both nodded, their faces shining with pride. "Excellent. Be in the main hall by twelve fifteen to set up. Competition begins at one o'clock sharp, lunch afterward."

"As you know, Virginia," Belle said, "we are without tomatoes." She put her arms around the girls' shoulders. "But we're excited to represent our county in stories and song."

Virginia closed her notebook. "Your leader is smart," she said to the girls. "Celebrate what you've achieved. And be respectful of the achievements of others."

Belle was delighted to see the girls nodding at Virginia's words. She immediately relaxed. She couldn't wait to get a good night's sleep on a luxury pillow. Tomorrow would come quickly and was ripe with promise—a chance to finally compete.

And, if he got her telegram and responded as she hoped he would, she'd have a chance to enjoy a long-overdue reunion with Boone.

Chapter 30

Belle slept so well that she awoke refreshed at sunrise and padded out to the veranda, where she watched the fiery orange ball ascend opposite a serene blue bay. After the girls got up, the three of them then indulged in a hearty breakfast in the hotel dining room, complete with soft-boiled eggs presented in petite silver cups that Fae dubbed *dreamy*. During the meal, they chatted with other club members hailing from Florida's top to its tip. And then the work began.

"Feed the string through the slats, Fae," Belle said. They were now both standing on chairs set beside tall interior shutters in the spacious show hall. The late-morning sun was streaming through two large windows as they attempted to hang their banner.

"I'll let you know when it's straight," Mazie offered from the floor, several yards away.

The girls were already wearing their competition dresses because Belle wasn't sure they'd have time to change after setting up. Clearly, keeping their white dresses clean was a lofty goal, but the sisters could at least try.

When they'd first arrived, Belle had walked around with

the girls, knowing the other booths would seem intimidating. *Celebrate what you've achieved. Be respectful of the achievements of others.* Virginia's advice to the sisters would truly be tested by their spin around the room, and that had been Belle's intent.

"Our banner is so plain," Fae had lamented as she'd watched the Manatee County girls hanging their pendant-style triangle.

"Just remember how much fun you had with your uncle Clay and aunt Edwina making ours," Belle had said. Fae's face had lit up at the memory.

The booths in the hall were thoughtfully arranged and packed with canned tomatoes. Some girls had stacked their wares on tiered shelves that stood up to six feet high. Baskets and crates full of fresh tomatoes were propped up sideways so passersby had an easy view of the plump red gems.

"Maybe these girls had trouble with their crop, too," Mazie had wondered aloud as they surveyed Hernando County's booth. Glass jars were displayed with an array of canned and pickled fruits and vegetables—peaches, string beans, and corn.

"And they showed up anyway, just like us," Belle had said, staying positive.

Now their banner was hung, too, and the trio stood back to admire it, proud to announce that Lee County had arrived. Next, Belle surprised the girls with a festive tablecloth to drape over the display table.

"Oh, look at the baby tomatoes!" Fae exclaimed when she saw it. Amelia had fringed a white cotton cloth with fuzzy red pom-poms.

Mazie helped Belle spread the special cloth over their table. "I sure like the Circle Club, Miss Belle," she said, and checked all sides to make sure it was evenly hung.

The booth next to theirs was impressive. Brevard County had come to compete. Cans of tomatoes were stacked on the floor in a square formation, layer upon layer rising toward the ceiling like a metal pyramid. Large baskets of fresh flowers adorned the club's two tables, which were covered with as many as twenty booklets. A girl in red knee socks stopped arranging flowers to address Fae and Mazie.

"I'm Ethelee Scott and I'm going home with those prizes." The girl nodded toward a cow and two calves munching on hay in a corner of the exhibition hall. "My club's bigger and better than yours."

Belle stopped herself from offering a firm retort. Mazie was busy wiping a smudge off her dress, and Fae was frozen, her hands in midair, retying her booklet's ribbon.

"Did you hear me?" the girl said, resuming work on her lush bouquet.

Fae dropped her hands and stood up straighter. "You go right ahead, Ethelee. We're not allowed to take cows on the boat, but we can surely carry home a cut-glass bowl."

Belle turned her back to Ethelee and mouthed "Yes!" to Fae. Earlier, they'd walked by the premium prize, sparkling on a pedestal. Though Belle had explained to the girls that without tomatoes they could only win ribbons, she was delighted to hear Fae stick up for her team and forgave her fibbing.

Ethelee glared at Fae and then walked toward the back of her club's elaborate booth, yanking up her socks.

• • •

Finally, the time had arrived, and a pair of judges began to approach each booth and evaluate displays. The man and woman who oversaw the competition leafed through booklets and listened as club members performed their signature songs. Other competitors were quiet, gauging their chances against the presenting club. Parents and friends were allowed to applaud from seats arranged in the center of the large room.

Belle spotted Virginia sitting in the front row next to the Florida home demonstration agent, a wavy-haired woman sporting a brooch that matched her earrings. Both women clapped after each performance, no doubt proud of every willing participant in the unique and burgeoning movement.

"We're getting close, girls," Belle said quietly. The Empire cut of her dress squeezed her ribs as she drew in a deep breath.

When the Big Two walked up to their table, the man announced, "Lee County." Belle was hovering well behind the girls, who stood next to each other. Their white cotton dresses were identical, right down to the scalloped hems. Green ribbons dangled from Fae's pigtails and Mazie's French braid.

"So far the smallest club we've seen," the thin woman noted. Her floor-length dress was royal blue and elegant, with flared sleeves. Its laced-up bodice covered her small breasts, a U-shaped neckline exposing her tanned chest. A white silk scarf completed the stylish outfit.

The man beside her was obese and sweaty. His bow tie peeked out from the folds of his beefy neck. "No one's counting, darling," he said, softly.

The girls offered the judges their booklets. Fae's cover featured two painted tomatoes, one whole and one sliced. Mazie had water-colored *1889* on hers. Both included the slogan "To make the best better."

Fae addressed the judges, her voice strong. "Our crop died and so did our parents, but as you'll read in our booklets, we're determined to always show up."

Mazie nodded but stayed silent. She slowly slid her hand up to cover the smudge on her dress.

"Sympathy doesn't factor into our judging," the woman sniped. She looked beyond the girls to Belle and stared at her.

The man ran a yellowed kerchief across his upper lip and then tucked it back into his pants pocket. "This is the point where we normally taste something, but why don't we move on to your song."

Holding hands, the girls began to sing, their tone clear and sweet. "In our fertile one-tenth acre, blessed with sunshine by our maker . . ."

As she listened, Belle examined the mean woman. Something about her was familiar.

"Despite our loss we persevere, we'll do our best again next year . . ."

Squinting, Belle focused on the woman's scarf, tied in a side knot. When her memory kicked in, her heart sank.

"That'll do," the woman snapped, interrupting the sisters. She grabbed the man's arm, pulling him toward the next booth.

The girls' voices trailed off and they stood silently, waiting. The first to respond was Virginia. She stood up and rallied the crowd to applaud along with her. Fae and Mazie curtsied and then waved at the audience.

Standing behind the girls, Belle clapped heartily, too, despite what she'd just pieced together.

• • •

Following the judging, conversations during the luncheon ranged from the hotel's running water to rumors that Mark Twain was staying there. The place settings were something to chat about, too—large plate, medium plate, small plate on top. Multiple forks and spoons completed the formal set. Fae and Mazie had gobbled up every course and now inspected chocolate sponge cakes set before them. Piped whipped cream ringed the round confections.

"I can't eat it, it's so beautiful," Fae marveled.

"I'll eat it," Mazie said, and reached for her sister's plate.

Fae whacked her hand. "*My* cake."

Belle had eaten her lunch but was now distracted, checking the room for Boone.

"Make sure to turn in your booklets, ladies." A woman circled the room behind the diners, announcing the reminder.

Prizes for first, second, and third place would be delivered through the mail, as judges would need time to read through the booklets. The award for best booth, however, had already been announced. Lee County was not surprised and not at all pleased.

"I hope that cow plops all over her shoes," Fae said, staring at a small crowd in the corner. Ethelee Scott was petting her club's hooved prizes and being interviewed by someone scribbling on a notepad.

Belle allowed herself to laugh; the girls had conducted themselves so well during the trip.

Suddenly, someone's hands were on Belle's shoulders. "Look who I found," Virginia said. Before Belle could swivel in her chair, the girls popped up from theirs.

"Mr. Boone!" Fae and Mazie yelled, abandoning their desserts to go hug him.

Boone wrapped his arms around the girls' shoulders. "Last time I saw you ladies you were slinging manure. Now look at ya!" The girls giggled and then regaled him with highlights of their trip.

"All right, girls," Virginia said after a few minutes, gently steering them back to their seats. "There'll be plenty of time on the ride home to talk about fancy closets and clothes presses." She nodded at Belle and offered a suggestion. "There's a brand-new wooden sidewalk outside the hotel."

Belle got up from her seat and turned toward Boone. "Are you hungry?" she asked, hoping he'd already eaten.

Immediately he said no. "But I'd like to stretch my legs."

Eager to spend time alone with Boone, Belle made sure the girls were settled and was pleased when a girl from another county took her seat and began talking to them.

Boone took Belle's hand and led her away from the table toward the lobby. When they walked by a broad wooden pillar, he whisked her behind it and shielded their faces with his hat. "I can't wait any longer to kiss you," he whispered. She let him, inhaling familiar scents—a mix of leather and gulf air. She pressed her body against his, lost in their kiss. With a callused hand, he gently clasped her face, drawing her parting lips closer to his. Nothing else mattered, worry melted away. They could finally love each other freely, no longer separated by lies and miles. Their warm kiss ended in a long, deep embrace.

When they finally parted, Belle said, "Let's go outside."

They exited the DeSoto and headed to the sidewalk that ran along Sarasota Bay. Countless fishing boats were in the water, either docked or heading out to sea.

"I'm sorry, Belle. I know the letters you found seemed devastating." Boone was walking backward in front of her. "But they were actually the key to opening up our future together."

She took his hands and pulled him toward a wooden table and benches next to the walkway. "You're going to trip and fall like that. Let's sit down."

After they did, Boone began to share the sequence of events that had led to Tilly admitting she'd lied about Boone being Wyatt's father. When his grief-stricken mother had confided in Tilly that Boone had accidentally shot and killed Daniel, Tilly had been shocked, having assumed Daniel had only left town but would soon return home. Upon learning the truth, she'd panicked and lied, claiming that Boone was her baby's father, because she was scared to raise a child alone.

"You must be hurt," Belle said. She couldn't imagine the

whirlwind of emotions Boone had weathered during his trip home. "Your brother . . ."

Boone interrupted. "Yeah, it's messy. But like my pa said, 'We need to get out of this jail.'"

Belle reached up and removed Boone's straw hat. She brushed curls off his forehead. "How *are* your parents?" Surely the family was reeling from their intense reunion.

"Well, we're talking, which is a good start." He ran both hands through his freed crown of hair. "Did I tell you my pa pummeled me?"

Belle noted a purple smudge on his cheek. "Make you feel a little bit better?"

He nodded. "I think my visit did us all some good."

Belle fiddled with the hat in her hands. "And Tilly?" She hoped Boone would be honest with her about the ribbon girl. The girl who'd nearly caused her to ransack his boat.

"Tilly will stay in Kissimmee with Wyatt. My mother's forgiven her for lying. She says innocent babies and desperate mothers can make for bad decisions." He shrugged. "Tilly never really meant anything to me in a way that would last. And she only matters now as my nephew's ma."

Belle grinned. "That makes sense." And it did. After all, how could she do anything but believe the man who'd locked himself up so they could be free to love each other?

Boone scooted closer to Belle on the bench. "Enough about me. What happened with the tomatoes? I'm sorry I couldn't be there to help."

Belle shrugged. "Something killed them . . . all of them. I've never seen anything like it."

"So, what did you bring to the show?" Boone asked.

Belle smiled. "Two brave girls." She took Boone's hand and stood up. "C'mon. Let's walk. I'll tell you all about it."

Chapter 31

Fae and Mazie and Belle and Boone had all returned from Sarasota more than a week ago, and the dining room in Baker's provided a perfect place for the girls and their supporters to gather. The afternoon was gorgeous and had sent boarders out into the sunshine to explore or relax on a sandy shore. Seats usually occupied by guests were now filled with friends and family, including the older Dawsons.

"Edwina, if you pour the tea, I'll get the muffins out of the oven," Abigail said. She scurried into the kitchen.

Everyone raised their cups to make the task easier for Edwina, but the girls covered theirs, holding out for milk.

"I see you brought the news with you, Belley," Merle said, eyeing a large piece of mail on the table. "But let's wait for Abigail."

Belle didn't want to open the "news," but there was no way around it. Everyone had insisted on being together for the big reveal.

"Mmm," Fae said. "I smell those muffins."

Mazie took a whiff of the air. "Lemon?"

"No, silly," Fae said. "Blueberry."

Abigail walked into the room carrying a tin full of baked goods. "New combination. Lemon blueberry!" she announced.

The girls looked at each other, jaws agape, delighted by their good guesses and Abigail's scrumptious experiment.

Edwina was sitting beside Clay. "We're still enjoying the girls' stories from the competition. That hotel sounds extraordinary."

Abigail took a seat and removed her oven mitts. "Please don't mention that to my boarders," she joked.

Clay held out his plate toward Abigail. "I'll bet you can't get a better muffin at that stuffy place."

Abigail beamed. "This man knows how to get himself the very biggest one." She served Clay a whopper.

Boone walked into the room, looking disheveled and wiping his hands on a dish towel. "Sorry I'm late. Decker's still getting back at me for being gone so long." He slumped down into a chair. "Mmm. Muffins."

Belle cleared her throat and reached for the packet. "As you may know, we've received our items back from Sarasota."

The girls started bouncing in their seats.

Edwina set down her teacup. "We're proud of you girls no matter what." Clay agreed through a mouthful of muffin.

With no way to avoid revealing the results, Belle got right to it. She opened the envelope and pulled out the two club booklets. When she saw the covers, she cringed. Both were stamped "Disqualified" big enough for all to see.

Mazie stopped bouncing. "My dang smudge."

Fae sat still, too. "I sure hope Ethelee Scott doesn't hear about this."

"'Disqualified'?" Abigail said, leaning over the table to get a better look. "Hogwash!"

"What are the show rules, Belle?" Merle asked, putting his arm around Mazie.

Belle knew the rules weren't the issue. She leafed through

Fae's book, and when she reached the last page, her concerns were confirmed. She looked up at the group. "The judges are a very prominent husband and wife in Sarasota." She read the names slowly. "Edward and Scarlet Smeltzer."

"Smeltzer . . . ," Boone said, rubbing his chin.

Abigail scratched her head. "Smeltzer . . ."

Edwina and Clay stayed quiet.

Merle slapped the table. "Smeltzer. Is she the onion lady?!"

Belle raised an eyebrow. "Yep."

Boone and Abigail pointed at each other. "The vulture!"

Belle added, "And the bird-scarf bandit."

The Dawson clan looked completely confused. "Who is this onion vulture bandit?" Clay asked, tying his napkin around his face like an outlaw.

Everyone burst out laughing.

When Belle caught her breath, she said, "Oh, Smeltzer, *Shmeltzer*. We showed up in Sarasota, and that makes us winners."

The others began to cheer, and the girls popped up from their seats. They paraded around the table, singing their tomato song, Merle directing with his butter knife.

Chapter 32

From the reaction Belle's outstretched finger elicited, one would have thought she were wearing a sparkling diamond ring, not one made with wire and a button. It had been several days since the banned booklets arrived, and the ladies of the Circle Club were now hovering over the ring and rehashing details of the proposal that Belle had already shared with them.

"Tell us again how Boone broke down crying," Sadie said, elbowing Amelia.

Belle laughed right along with the others. "He did not," she said.

The women were sitting on blankets outside Belle's cottage, close to Baker's so Abigail could easily join them if time allowed.

"You should have known something big was about to happen the minute Boone showed up in clean clothes," Poppy said. "When Mitchell shaved his beard, I knew."

"That's a good tip," Paulette said, smoothing her lace collar. She and Duke were still spending time together after several months, a new record for her.

Nearly two weeks had passed since Belle and Boone's

reunion at the DeSoto, and—wanting to share a joyous secret for once—they'd spent all that time keeping their engagement news to themselves. But at last, they'd let everyone else know. They'd decided to say that they had gotten engaged on the grounds of the DeSoto during the competition, the hotel being a much more romantic setting than a tomato patch. The fib was harmless and kept them from having to explain why Boone had been so eager to propose before he left town. In Sarasota, Boone had admitted to Belle that he'd asked her when he did because, not knowing what awaited him back home, he'd wanted to make sure the bond they shared was even stronger than ever.

"Well, John Parker had better choose the *perfect* setting if he wants me to say yes," Hazel said, shielding her eyes from the sun.

"Oh please . . . ," Alice said. "He'd have you at 'Will you . . .'"

Hazel playfully pushed Alice over onto the blanket.

When the engagement talk subsided, Amelia asked about the competition. "How did the dresses hold up?"

Belle didn't have the heart to tell her about Mazie's smudge. "They were perfect, Amelia, and the girls loved the tomato tablecloth, too."

From across the lawn, the ladies saw Abigail heading toward them, walking as briskly as her buxom body would abide. She was breathing hard when she arrived. "What'd I miss?" Coconut scampered over and placed a paw on Abigail's skirt.

Sadie ticked off the recent topics on her fingers. "Boone's a crier, Hazel's a pushover, and we're about to talk about the disqualification."

Abigail bent over and fed the dog a piece of beef jerky from her apron pocket. "Don't bother with that last one. We never had a chance. Dirty judge." Upright again, still catching her breath from the effort, she looked over at Belle. "Did Boone really cry?"

"No!" Belle insisted.

Poppy patted her blanket, offering Abigail a seat. "No, thank you," Abigail said, scanning its surface as if looking for ants. Hooking her thumbs in her apron's neck strap, she announced, "I've got an idea for the club, ladies."

"Wedding planning!" Paulette said, practically singing.

"Of course," Abigail said. "But first?" She smiled. "First, we plan a tribute to all things tomato."

Chapter 33

Midnight was ticking toward the inky hours of early morning, and every bed in Baker's was filled . . . except for one. Abigail was at the property next door, outside Thomas Edison's laboratory. Hours ago, she'd been organizing a tomato festival with the Circle Club. Now she was squatting, using the light from a candle to search for a small turtle shell somewhere around her feet. Once she found it, she grabbed the key hidden underneath and inserted it into the lock on the lab door.

When the spring-loaded pins responded, she blew out the candle and slowly inched open the door. Of course there was no one inside, but the revered space still seemed occupied somehow, by ghosts of innovation, lurking and territorial. Slowly reaching inside, she searched for a light switch, her fingertips lightly sweeping the wall. Within a few seconds, she located a T-shaped handle to the left of the doorframe. Firing up the lights was risky, but necessary for Abigail to accomplish her mission.

With a turn of the handle, the black room gradually grew bright as bulbs slowly activated in lamps that hung above the large room. As they reached their brightest level, Abigail was reminded of an article that had appeared in the *New York World*. After watching Edison reenact illuminating his laboratory for the first time, the reporter had written that the bulbs "finally burst out to obscure even the brilliant sun of Fort Myers." The room was now quite "brilliant" indeed.

She'd have to work as quickly as she could before someone spotted the glowing lab.

The configuration of the space was familiar to Abigail. Three years ago, while the Edisons were up north, she'd snuck into the lab and smuggled out a bundle of copper wire to create a unique gadget—one that, ultimately, didn't work. That is, not until last year, when Belle accidentally found it inside Baker's storage shed.

Miraculously, the machine had fired up when Belle cranked its handle, but it performed in a way that Abigail never intended. Her goal had been to create a more compact telephone for use on desks; instead, the device intercepted active phone calls in New York City. When Abigail happened upon Belle listening to a conversation on her contraption, she'd been forced to admit that she'd been an inventor before moving to Fort Myers, and that she'd relocated after losing a heartbreaking lawsuit against a Boston machinist who'd stolen her design for an improved paper-bag machine.

The revelation had left Belle astonished and Abigail ashamed of her trespass. After dismantling the device and returning the wire, she had vowed to never again step foot inside the lab. But now here she was again, both feet firmly planted on the wooden floorboards.

Thankfully and extraordinarily, this time she'd entered with Mr. Edison's blessing *and* instructions on how to finally bring electricity to the main street of Fort Myers. The evolution of events had been unexpected but logical. In the last year, she'd simply grown weary of hearing frustrated townspeople bad-mouth their famous neighbor. Then, as she'd begun to consider how to solve the problem, she'd realized that *she* was the answer—or would be, if only she could gain access to the laboratory.

And so, she'd officially offered her expertise to Edison. Her only request had been to remain anonymous; she'd explained that she valued her standing in the community as a respected business owner and had no ambitions beyond that.

Ultimately, a collaboration had simply made the most sense. After all, with her innovative brain and background, why wouldn't she attempt to revive Edison's glowing reputation *and* the dynamo?

Now, standing in the laboratory, Abigail took a moment to survey the wide room. She inhaled the scent of mildew and latex. Summer rains had leached into the windowsills, and daily heat had warmed the dozens of rubber hoses dangling down into glass beakers arranged on long metal tables. Pulleys hung from the ceiling, and countless bottles of chemicals filled the shelves of tall cabinets lined up along one wall. Table saws, lathes, and cans of engine oil sat on the floor: a still life left behind after Edison's most recent project. Visible inside a small side room was the narrow cot where Edison reportedly took five-to-ten-minute catnaps. A straw boater's hat wrapped with a black band hung from a hook. Uneven stacks of thick notebooks bordered the bed like a paper forest.

Abigail closed her eyes and crossed her arms over her chest, considering the moment. Why on earth had she followed the impulse to offer her help with the dynamo? Had she been acting out of a desire to help Edison and Fort Myers, or had she wanted to get herself back into this incredible lab? Either way, there she was, holding a packet mailed discreetly to her by Thomas Alva Edison himself.

She opened her eyes and looked around for a pair of

dynamos. She knew that Edison had already activated one of the machines to light up his personal property. The other—her target—was not operating.

Spotting one generator right away in what she recalled was the machine shop area, she walked over to it. After examining the device for several minutes, she determined that this dynamo was already hooked up and powering electricity to the lab and to Seminole Lodge. As she looked around for the second dynamo, she squelched a burning desire to explore every inch of this fascinating space. *Stay focused,* she told herself.

Within a minute or two, she located the dormant dynamo tucked in a corner atop a sturdy wooden table. It was about the height of two stacked citrus crates and had a heavy metal base. Its long horizontal armature would soon begin rotating if all went as planned. On top of the shaft were two identical field coils that looked like oversized spools of thread. Both were wrapped in wire.

Abigail dragged a chair next to the dynamo and opened Edison's packet. Then she pulled out the contents and ran her fingers over the paperwork, held recently in the hands of a genius. Edison had enclosed both a letter and several pages of instructions titled "Direct Current Dynamo." Edison's handwriting was vertical and legible, not the more popular slanted, sweeping style.

> *Dear Miss Baker—*
> *The enclosed instructions should "amply" guide you on powering up the dynamo.*

Abigail grinned at his wordplay.

> *I received your note outlining your background as an inventor, complete with blueprints*

for your machine to produce flat-bottomed paper bags. Quite impressive.

Your generous offer to assist me comes at an ideal time, as I am desperate to fulfill at least one overdue promise. Seems my world is a snarl of loose ends and unfinished business these days.

I certainly understand your request to keep our collaboration a secret to safeguard your privacy. While some may accuse me of courting publicity, the fact is my near deafness has—thankfully—liberated me from the riotous clatter of celebrity. You have my word that I will stay silent on the matter.

Creating a mystery around how electricity lit up Front Street will also sell endless copies of the Press, *an additional win for the city. I can see Fitz's clever headline now: "Watt Happened?!"*

Thank you in advance for your help, Miss Baker. I wish you success and satisfaction as you clandestinely dabble in a former passion. Should all go as planned, I look forward to seeing paradise bathed in brightness when we next visit.

Yours sincerely,
Thomas A. Edison

Abigail noted his showy signature. The top on the letter *T* arched up and over the entire name, stopping just beyond the *n* in *Edison*—the creative flare of a world-renowned luminary.

She set aside the letter and began reviewing the detailed step-by-step instructions. Her hands shook slightly as she absorbed the importance of the actions she was about to undertake: collaborating with Thomas Edison, ushering her town into "the Electric Age," and keeping both these developments a secret. She drew several deep breaths to calm herself.

First, she studied the dynamo. The top of the machine featured a rectangular plaque that read "Edison Machine Works." Below that, "Schenectady, NY" was printed in raised letters along with "No. 353." She read that the dynamo's capacity was five kilowatts at 125 volts, information that was also stamped on the machine. Edison's notes provided all the details she needed about the switches, circuit boards, meters, and regulators required to run the DC dynamo, which was driven by an Armington & Sims reciprocating engine in combination with a Babcock & Wilcox steam-driven boiler. This information was exhilarating! She'd forgotten how much she had enjoyed science before leaving it behind for a stove. She set to work, and with every wire she connected, every contact she tested, it was as if her mind itself were glowing like an incandescent bulb.

By nearly four o'clock in the morning, Abigail had completed each of the steps required to get the dynamo up and running. All she had left to do was yank a large handle on the right side of the machine. But before she did, she mentally ran through the exit plan she'd formulated earlier.

Main Street was a mile away, so she'd have to make her escape without knowing whether she'd achieved her goal. If she was successful and the lights on Front Street lit up, it wouldn't take Fitz long to show up at the lab in search of a scoop on the biggest story of his professional life. She'd estimated that the *Press* editor could run to the Edison property in twenty minutes or ride a horse in ten after he got it saddled up. Heck, he might just thunder toward the property riding bareback.

Either way, she'd have to skedaddle out of the lab and over to Baker's as soon as she powered up the dynamo. Her role as "undercover tinkerer" needed to remain known only to her and Belle—even though she'd never intended for anyone else to know.

Her palm sweaty from humidity and anticipation, Abigail grabbed the handle. She crossed her fingers on the other hand, closed her eyes, and yanked. And with that, the mystery of "Watt Happened?" was—she hoped—underway.

• • •

Within seconds of her attempt to rev up the dynamo, Abigail had shut off the lights, locked the lab door, and scurried across the yard toward Baker's, using her candle to guide her home. Now she was tucked under the covers, wearing her robe and crocheted nightcap, wide awake in the dark, heart racing. In her haste, she'd forgotten to check the pocket watch on her nightstand, but she didn't dare light another candle now. She guessed perhaps five or six minutes had passed since she'd left the lab.

Had the lights kicked on along Front Street? Had they woken up Merle in his bedroom over Duggan's? Were all the roosters downtown crowing right now? Unable to take the suspense, she got up and crawled to the window. Slowly, she pulled back the curtain ever so slightly and peered out into the blackness, the new moon invisible and unhelpful in her search for clues. After several minutes of squinting toward the lab, Abigail spied the glow of a kerosene lamp in the distance. Fitz?! She let the curtain drop and quickly crawled back into bed. Did Fort Myers finally have electricity? She felt proud and nervous and astounded all at the same time.

Before long, Abigail heard tapping on her bedroom window. Fitz was lurking outside! *Tap, tap, tap.* She rolled herself out of bed and straightened her cap. She did her best to look sleepy and parted the curtains.

"Merle!" she said to the face in the glowing lamplight.

He began nodding at a panicked pace and motioned for her to let him in, which she attempted to do.

"You won't believe it!" he exclaimed and practically climbed through the half-open window before getting stuck.

She rubbed her eyes for effect and said, "Honey, come around to the front door."

Once they were both inside the kitchen, she fired up her own kerosene lamp so they could better see each other. No need to pretend anymore that she was asleep.

"Front Street is lit up like it's high noon, Abigail! We've got electricity!" He took her hand and spun her around below his raised arm.

"Merle, shh. And slow down. I'm barely awake." She moved the coffeepot to a warm spot on the stove. "How is that even possible?"

Before he could answer, Fitz flew through the kitchen door. "Is he here? Where is he?" The newsman was gasping for air.

Abigail shushed him, too, and whispered, "My boarders are sleeping!"

Merle took Fitz's hand and spun him just like he had Abigail. "Wheeeee! We have electricity!"

Fitz ripped his hand away. "Why are you two awake?" He paced around the kitchen, opening cabinets and checking under the dinette. "The lab is dark. Seminole Lodge is dark. The only thing lit up is Front Street! Are you hiding Edison, Abigail?"

She said softly but firmly, "I'm not hiding anything, Fitz." Stoking embers inside the stove's firebox, she added, "I've got coffee on."

"Coffee? This calls for tonsil paint!" Merle exclaimed, grabbing glasses and a bottle of whiskey off the counter. He poured shots, and he and Fitz knocked them back. Abigail declined.

"Augie's getting the press ready for a special edition, but

we need some facts!" Fitz said, referring to his sixteen-year-old apprentice. "Abigail, did you see anything? Anything at all."

"Just the inside of my eyelids, Fitz." Abigail poured herself a cup of lukewarm coffee. "I need to get dressed and see this for myself before my boarders wake up to all of this hullabaloo."

Fitz held up his finger. "Boone!" He raced out the door.

Abigail shook her head. "That's risky."

Merle kissed Abigail on the cheek. "I'll make sure Boone doesn't shoot Fitz, and I'll wake up Belley." He snagged the whiskey bottle and his kerosene lamp and headed out toward the dock.

Abigail collapsed into a chair and sighed. *I guess I haven't lost my touch,* she thought and peeled off her nightcap, smiling ear to ear.

• • •

The scene along Front Street was astounding no matter where you looked. Above, incandescent lamps twinkled in a dazzling display of innovation, electric stars in a black sky. On the ground, an impromptu party was underway—and growing.

When Abigail, Merle, Belle, and Boone arrived at 4:45 a.m., the street was full of energy. A boy was juggling lemons atop his pony, neighbors in nightclothes waved hand-painted signs that read "Let there be light!" Dozens of tables were covered with casseroles, cured hams, and corn pones. One woman was setting out lemon pies that looked like little suns enclosed in crust. Neighbors were more than happy to share food they'd already prepared for their Sunday dinner.

Merle elbowed Abigail and pointed toward a small crowd. "Clay's over there taking orders for shutters!" The Everetts, one of several families who lived below the glare, were first in line.

"Free Jolts! Free Jolts!" Billy Berg shouted to the crowd. He owned the local saloon and was handing out specialty shots—bourbon mixed with lemonade. "Let's get Jolted, folks!"

Captain Al Metzger, who skippered one of the region's mail boats, took two. "I don't make runs on Sundays," he reassured those around him. He then downed both shots, starboard hand first, then portside.

Boone and Belle looked at each other and shrugged. "Over here, Billy!" Boone shouted and waved both arms to get his attention.

As everyone rejoiced, one distraught woman scurried through the crowd, clutching a rooster in each arm. Both birds had a strip of fabric wrapped around their eyes like a blindfold. "Night, night, boys," she cooed and hurried off into the darkness.

When the Fort Myers Band arrived, Merle helped the Cooper twins and the rest of the band set up on Duggan's porch. He poured a shot for each member—and one for himself—and they all raised their glasses and toasted toward the lights. One man drank the shot out of his trombone's detached mouthpiece, his thumb plugging the shank.

When the band finally started playing, couples were drawn into an off-key but spirited waltz. Hazel and John Parker paired up, as did Poppy and Pastor Peck. Belle and Boone just watched for now. Suddenly, Norville Decker spun by, twirling one woman across the road, now a makeshift dance floor, then reaching for another. Boone stared at the gangly caretaker and his giddy partner. He leaned over to Belle. "Wait. Is Decker attractive?"

Belle clapped along with the music and answered with a shrug. "Who's to say?"

Even the Cravins were waltzing, Ida leading, of course. She moved forward and back with her nose in the air, appearing to gaze at the lights but fooling no one who knew this to be the usual position of her nose. Ida's arrogance was as predictable as the countless squares being carved in the sand from the box step.

Nearby, Fitz was busy polling the crowd, angling for clues, as determined as a fisherman casting a net. His latest haul was Oscar and Jeannie Powell.

"I swear on my telegraph I had nothing to do with this!" Oscar insisted, his palm raised.

"Bottom's up, Fitz!" Jeannie said, offering him a Jolt and downing one of her own.

On this momentous morning, the townspeople of Fort Myers were elated—and quite drunk. Even as nature's light bulb began to glow in the east, the party raged on.

"I hate to leave, but I need to get breakfast made," Abigail said, as she and Boone sidled up on either side of a tipsy Merle, their arms looped through his.

Boone craned his head back toward Belle, who was walking behind them. "It's almost lights out for Merle," he told her, grinning.

Belle chuckled and thought about this boozy and historic day in Fort Myers. *Who had lit up those lamps?* How would lights change their town? She looked forward to reading today's newspaper and wondered as she walked.

Is my hunch about how we got electricity even close to right?

• • •

Augie had already dropped off the *Press*'s special edition, and Abigail was watching her guests pore over copies as she moved in and out of the dining room, serving breakfast. Boarders had slept through the breaking news and were eager to read about what they'd missed. Abigail tried to peek at the articles as she refilled coffee cups.

"We're vacationing right in the heart of history, Girdy!" a Pennsylvania man declared, nudging his wife so hard she dropped her fork.

"And you snored right through it, Joseph," she said, plucking the utensil out of her scrambled eggs.

A young boy turned toward his father. "Will there be another party tonight, Papa?"

Ruffling his son's hair, the burly man said, "If there is, you can stay up for a bit of it."

The boy beamed and chugged his orange juice.

Abigail surveyed the dining room and determined that everyone was set for now. She slipped back into the kitchen and grabbed a newspaper from a stack on the floor. Sitting at the dinette, she smoothed the front page and began to read the main article.

IN THE DARK ABOUT THE LIGHT!

A four-year-old promise to Fort Myers has been kept! In the wee hours of Sunday morning, the long-dormant lamps lining both sides of Front Street exploded with light!

SOMEHOW, electricity generated from Thomas Edison's laboratory zipped along underground cables placed by the Lamplighters and then shot up lines leading to the lamps. ZAPPO! A dazzling display of electricity lit up our town's hub, waking all who were suddenly bathed in light at approximately four o'clock this morning.

"My goats started bleating for breakfast," said Butch Rowe, who lives behind Cravin & Company. "I looked at the clock and couldn't make no sense of it."

Neither can we! This publication remains perplexed as to how this development transpired. NO evidence of Thomas Edison arriving in Fort Myers has surfaced. Captains of all schooners deny transporting our illustrious neighbor; no one reports renting him any form of transportation. The lab and Seminole Lodge were pitch-black upon inspection. In addition, our trusted neighbor Oscar Powell confirms he was not involved in bringing the dynamo to life BUT says he did previously install a light switch in his office.

"During his visit two years ago, Mr. Edison provided me the switch and advised me on how to install it," Powell explained. "I accepted the responsibility to turn the lights on and off each evening and morning whenever he hooked up the lights. And starting today, I will!"

The WHODUNIT was of no concern to revelers during a spontaneous and spirited party that broke out predawn under the lights.

"Sure, I had one too many Jolts," admitted Mary Hilbert, "but we've been waiting for four years to celebrate! I did make it to church."

Amen, Mary!

Next, we await answers to two important questions:

Will our homes and businesses one day be blessed with electricity?

Will Mr. Edison respond to our telegram requesting comment about his role in this incredible development?

Be assured, we are on the case. (Tipsters, welcome!)

Until next time, dear readers.

Abigail looked up from the exciting article. "Whodunit?" She gave a little nod of satisfaction. "*I* dunnit."

Chapter 34

Hunched over the counter in Duggan's, Merle poured himself a third cup of coffee, hoping to dull the headache for which he had only himself to blame. Too much celebrating. His breakfast covered some of the *Press*, so he pushed aside the plate of toast and a sticky jar of mulberry jam. He then began reading the front-page article.

THE WIZARD WON'T SAY!

Western Union man Oscar Powell delivered a series of telegrams to the *Press* directly from the esteemed—and enigmatic—Thomas A. Edison. The following is, in part, his response to our request for an explanation of how Fort Myers became electrified without his presence here.

"I have my muckers working beside me in the New Jersey complex, but I have collaborators operating all over the world. (You may recall that Professor James Ricalton—who spent time in Fort Myers last winter recuperating—traveled the Orient on my behalf, searching for a bamboo species to improve the filament in my incandescent light bulbs.) Four years ago, I promised to personally light up the town in my beloved 'Eden,' but obstacles to do so have been many and momentous. Therefore, I prevailed upon others for help to get the job done."

Regrettably, Edison did NOT identify the collaborator or collaborators who helped realize his promise to our town. Instead, he proffered the following:

"Why would I subject my support in the South to the understandable scrutiny of curious neighbors and a diligent press? I'm accustomed to both but will not expose those I respect and rely on to such intense encounters."

OUR INVITATION: The *Press* bids any and all collaborators to come forward. We extend our solemn promise to handle interviews and coverage with the utmost respect and professionalism.

Stand by, readers.

When the bell jingled above Duggan's front door, Merle

looked up from the paper, pleased to see Abigail. He immediately apologized for his excesses at the celebration.

"I'm sorry," he said, rubbing his temples. "Can't seem to shake this headache. I'm a fool."

Abigail sauntered over to him and kissed him on the cheek. "But you're *my* fool." She smiled and took a bite of his toast.

"You're in a good mood," Merle said, and sipped his coffee.

"Between the electricity and the engagement, what's not to be happy about?" Abigail said. She took a seat at the counter across from Merle and dragged his plate of toast toward her.

"Good point, my gal. Two *major* developments. Now I don't blame myself anymore for celebrating . . . a lot." He reached over and slathered his toast—now hers—with jam. "How about our Belley . . ."

Abigail wiped her hands on her apron. "I know. She and Boone have a wonderful future ahead." She sat quietly for a moment.

Merle leaned forward and spun his fingers around both ears. "Are the wheels turning? Already have the wedding planned?" He winked at her.

"You got me. I was baking a cake for a second there . . ." Abigail smiled, twisted on the stool, and slid off the seat. She walked over to the produce baskets and grabbed a tomato with each hand. Turning back toward Merle, she said, "I shared an idea with the Circle Club." She held up the tomatoes.

Merle stood and walked around the counter. "Those'll be five cents, ma'am."

Abigail continued. "We're organizing a tomato festival. The Dawson girls can talk up their club to our town's other young ladies, and who doesn't like tomatoes?"

Merle began checking inventory in the barrels and bins that were set up in the center of the store. "Tell me more, honey."

"Well, neighbors will contribute whatever they'd like," Abigail explained. "Margie can bring her breaded tomatoes, and Dorene makes a delicious tomato spice cake." She began to follow Merle around. "Think about it. Stewed and creamed tomatoes, tomato casseroles, tomato jam, tomato sauce, tomato cheese bread . . ."

Merle held up a hand. "I'm sold, dear. What about a tomato pie–eating contest, too?" He began to restack cabbages, placing the purple heads on top of the green.

"Yes!" Abigail said. "And we can offer a substantial award."

Merle sighed when he got to a completely empty bin. "Look here. A few weeks ago, the Finnegan boys cleaned me out of penny candy." He shook his head. "I'm still waiting on a new shipment."

Abigail returned the tomatoes and walked over to check out the bare bin. "That's odd. Didn't you recently drop off the Helpful Hamper at the Finnegans'?"

"Yep. Doesn't make sense. All I know is, the boys somehow paid for two big bags of candy." Merle turned away from the bin and took Abigail in his arms. "I love your idea, honey." His hands slowly moved up her back as he squeezed her tight. "You know I looove tomatoes." He moved his body back and forth over her shapely front side.

Abigail pulled away and slapped his chest, smiling. "Shame on you, Squirrel!"

They both laughed and Merle led her back over to the counter. "Let's write down our ideas for the big festival." He was happy to help Abigail.

And, as the pounding in his head continued, he was even happier to sit back down.

Chapter 35

After more than a week of coordinating who would bring what, the town's residents had come together joyfully yet again, but this time to celebrate tomatoes. The electricity bash had featured plenty of drinking, but this afternoon the crowd was more interested in eating.

"Fill it to the rim, Caroline!" Merle said, his eyes on the dish being served up for him. He'd made the first stop on what would surely become a belly-busting stroll along Front Street, his tasks for Abigail complete. He was done hanging the Lee County Girls' Tomato Club banner across Duggan's porch, and he'd helped neighbors carry their offerings to tables set out in rows. Now he was focused on devouring a bowl of Caroline Dodd's spicy tomatoes and rice.

"Here's a leaflet, ladies," Amelia said, offering the information to passing neighbors. She and Sadie were standing behind a long table covered with the canning club literature Belle had brought back from Sarasota. Glass jars labeled "Saucy Sadie's" were lined up on the table, too.

"We've had a few takers," Sadie said to Amelia, who was

still holding the pamphlet, "but people are more interested in my tomato sauce." She shrugged. "I can't help how good it is."

Hazel was standing behind the table with her arms crossed. "I think the real problem is you-know-who."

Ida Cravin was walking back and forth in front of the Circle Club's table, holding a hand-painted sign featuring a large circle with a line through it. Below was the phrase "Can the clubs!" Pot-stirrer Etta Dunn was marching behind Ida, ripping up leaflets and yelling the three-word phrase. No one in the hungry crowd seemed to care. People were simply weaving around the pair on their way to snag the next treat.

"Hold still, dear, or your tomato will look like a wound," Poppy said, trying to paint a small red circle on the cheek of a squirming five-year-old boy. Behind him, a line of fidgeting children awaited their chance at tomato cheeks.

On the street in front of Dawson's shop, Paulette was singing "The Village Blacksmith," a poem by Longfellow that had been set to music. But no one in the crowd could hear her. The Fort Myers Band was playing so loudly that she appeared to be only mouthing the words. Lyrics like "the muscles of his brawny arms are strong as iron bands" didn't reach any ears, including those of the village blacksmith himself. Duke was standing between Paulette and the band, holding a tomato bacon sandwich in his soot-stained hands. When he caught her eye, she just shrugged, and they both began to laugh, more sounds that no one heard.

"Thank you, Mrs. Varga," Fae said to the woman standing in front of the cigar shop. The girl stuck her nose over a plate of biscuits and tomato gravy prepared by the shop owner's wife.

Mazie was right behind her and stepped forward so she could try some tomato gravy, too.

"The secret is bacon drippings," Mrs. Varga explained to folks in line, her cast-iron skillet brimming with the creamy pink sauce.

"Bacon made my tomato toast better, too!" Fae declared. Mazie nodded in agreement as she inhaled the hearty food.

"Looks like the festival is going well," Belle said, as she and Boone walked hand in hand along Front Street.

"Tell me again why we're celebrating something that died on you?" Boone said, playfully squeezing her hand.

Belle looked up at Boone. "Funny you should say that. I've got some news, but you can't tell anyone."

Boone steered her toward the steps of Duggan's, which was closed for the festival. They sat down. "Let's hear it."

Belle tapped her bootheels on the wooden step. "Abigail got the Finnegan boys to admit they killed our tomatoes."

Boone twisted toward her. "What?!"

"Shh," Belle said, and lowered her voice. "After Merle told Abigail that the boys bought all his candy, she pulled them aside one day when they were playing in the park. You know how Abigail can be . . . sweet but stern? She got the boys to confess that they were paid to cut the roots of all our tomato plants."

"Those little hoodlums!" Boone said angrily. "Who paid them?"

Belle told him the boys had quickly squealed on none other than Ida Cravin. They were mad at her because they got sick after eating so much candy. "It's upsetting," Belle said, "but they're just kids."

Boone shook his head. "That woman's awful. I think she wrote a letter to my parents and held back the one I wrote to them."

Belle took Boone's hand. "She *is* awful. The good news is, as hard as Ida tries to make everyone else miserable, she's the one who's always unhappy."

Boone groaned. "Still, I'd like to see her get a taste of her own medicine."

Belle stood and pulled Boone up. "Let's go. I think the pie-eating contest is starting soon."

Boone quickly added, "And there's a *significant* award."

Both began to laugh. They'd heard an excited Abigail hint at least a half-dozen times about some sort of big prize for the winner.

Chapter 36

When Belle and Boone spotted Abigail, she was setting out tomato pies across a long table. Sadie was trailing her, tearing basil leaves and dropping them into the open-faced pies. Others had told her the extra touch was unnecessary, but she'd insisted that the tastier the pies, the faster the contestants would eat them. Meanwhile, Merle was arranging chairs in front of the table and getting his hand slapped each time he reached for a nibble.

Boone elbowed Belle and gestured toward the end of the table. "What's Alice up to?"

Nearby, the young woman was jumping up and down, her alligator boots kicking up sand.

"Don't know," Belle said, and walked over to her friend. "Hey, Alice."

"Hi, Belle," Alice said, clapping her hands over her head, then slapping each thigh as they returned to center.

Belle watched Alice continue her steady rhythm.

Finally, Alice spoke, still panting. "I'm getting hungrier . . . and hungrier for the contest."

Belle grinned. "Keep it up." She walked back over to Boone.

"Well?" he asked.

"Alice is going to win the pie-eating contest," she said.

Boone crossed his arms. "I like Alice."

People began to gather near the pie table, curious about the competition, even as Ida and Etta continued their protest against women's clubs. Ignoring the droning pair, Hazel handed out glasses of lemonade to thirsty festival-goers.

"Go give this to your mother," Abigail instructed and set a full glass on Hazel's tray.

Hazel stared at Abigail, who smiled and made her eyebrows dance. Hazel did as she was told.

"All righty, folks," Abigail announced loudly. "In a few minutes, we'll start the pie-eating contest, featuring two prizes."

The crowd buzzed, speculating about what the prizes could be.

She held up an egg timer. "The challenge will last two minutes. Whoever finishes the most tomato pie in that time will win a significant award."

A little girl sitting on her father's shoulders yelled, "Oh, I hope it's a pony!"

Abigail laughed. "We've got six chairs to fill." She turned toward Alice, who was cooling down. "So far, Alice Bishop is number one."

"Number one!" Boone yelled and pumped his fist for Alice.

A man in the crowd shouted, "What's the prize?"

Others pleaded with Abigail. "Tell us!"

Slowly, Abigail bent over and picked up a smooth chunk of wood from under the table. She spoke as she eased her round body back up. "We're grateful to Mr. Ritter for carving one of our prizes for today's contest." She held it up. "A perfectly plump wooden tomato."

The Ritter tomato elicited tepid applause but drew at least one person to the contest table—a man dressed in overalls, smoking a corncob pipe. Alice took her seat at the opposite end.

"Now the significant award," Abigail said. "It's quite a unique opportunity." She paused to maximize the anticipation. The plot she'd cooked up after Merle suggested a contest was about to unfold. She'd been quite pleased when her request—vital to her plan—had been granted, most likely repayment for her recent success in the laboratory. She continued. "The winner of the tomato pie–eating contest will exchange letters with . . ." Abigail smiled and then announced enthusiastically, "With our *own* Mrs. Mina Edison!"

Gasps erupted from the crowd as some women squealed. Skirts swished and boots sprayed sand everywhere as people rushed toward the table. One woman, shoved by a neighbor, knocked the pipe out of the seated contestant's mouth. Another woman yelled, "Mina's mine!" as she elbowed others out of her way. Surveying the expected chaos, Abigail was not at all surprised to see Ida drop her sign like a hot poker and dash toward the pies. Hazel ran ahead of her mother, clearing a path, apparently having decided some sort of plan was underway after receiving her marching orders from Abigail.

When the dust finally cleared, all six seats were taken. Surprisingly, every pie remained on the table, fully intact. The overalled man was gone, pushed out somehow by the town's reedy, pale schoolteacher. Ida was sitting next to Alice, who was loosening her jaw, shifting it back and forth. In a rare move, Ida had removed her flamboyant picture hat, revealing coarse, mousy hair and her intense desire to win. The remaining seats were occupied by two women and a skinny red-haired boy. Poppy approached the youngster and offered her Bible to boost his bottom. He accepted and no one griped about the divine intervention, at least not out loud.

Abigail paced back and forth in front of the table as she delivered instructions. "Arms behind your back, contestants. No hands allowed." She studied Ida's face as she passed by and liked what she saw there. "Good luck, folks." She looked over at a band member she'd invited to the contest. "Randall, can we have a drum roll?"

Randall's face was serious, as if he and his snare drum had been hired for a grand event. The tip of his sticks began to vibrate, creating a tight roll. Abigail flipped the egg timer and shouted, "Eat those pies!"

The crowd started chanting, "Eat, eat, eat!" and moved closer to the table. The Circle Club cheered on Alice, whose pie was already minus a third of its outer crust and filling. The schoolteacher had chosen not to remove her glasses, likely an attempt to focus on her quarry. A piece of basil was stuck to one of the lenses.

Hazel stood next to Abigail and offered softly, "My mother looks . . . odd."

Abigail beamed. "Delicious, isn't it?" She checked the timer, which still housed most of its sand in the top bulb.

Ida's eyelids appeared heavy, and her chewing had grown labored. Beads of sweat rolled down her cheeks, streaking her thick makeup. The only contestant with more pie left than Ida was the little boy, who wouldn't stop waving at his mother.

Abigail knew that Ida was simply headed for a little nap, but she thought it best to get ahead of any potential concerns. "Keep in mind, folks, competing can be stressful," she said loudly, "especially with that exciting award on the line."

Her words seemed to energize the crowd even more, and the chanting grew louder.

"Halfway there!" Abigail yelled over the din. She smiled at the boy and pointed toward his pie. "Eat, honey," she advised.

While the sand quickly slid through the neck of the timer, the crowd focused on Alice and the schoolteacher. Each had nearly half a pie in her belly. Suddenly, though, all eyes turned toward Ida, who was clearly struggling. The woman's neck kept bowing under the weight of her head, which dipped closer and closer to the table. Eyes shut, she began to moan, battling whatever force was interfering with her quest to befriend Mina. Onlookers were spellbound, cheering each time she rebounded from a deep bob toward the pie. The fact that no one came to the woman's aid reflected how poorly she'd treated so many in town.

"Three, two . . . ," Abigail yelled, counting down, her fingers held up high.

It was on "one" that Ida's face finally landed in her pie, the direct hit launching red sauce and tomato chunks from both sides of the pan. The loud thud silenced the crowd, but not for long. When Abigail raised the arm of the contest winner, a raucous chant broke out. "Alice, Alice, Alice!"

The other contestants stopped their frantic feeding and began to wipe off their messy faces. The little boy hopped off his seat and congratulated Alice with a brief handshake before running back to his family. Ida was somehow snoring, her nose buried in tomato pie.

Belle nudged Boone. "What in the world? Could this be 'the taste of her own medicine' you were hoping for?"

He nodded and crossed his arms. "I have no idea what's going on, either. But whatever it is, it's a damn good start."

Abigail congratulated the contestants, thanked them all for competing, and then presented Alice with the wooden tomato and a folded note concealing Mina's address.

"I *knew* I could win," Alice exclaimed, beaming. "I'm a very good eater. Always have been." Stifling a burp, she collected her prizes and took a deep bow toward her enthusiastic fans.

The contest complete, onlookers headed back to the heart of the tomato festival along Front Street. While Ida slept, her cheek now pressed against the pie plate, Abigail and Hazel worked around her as they cleaned up the table. Boone and Merle offered to move the woman, but Hazel suggested they leave her marinating for a while.

"Maybe she'll wake up enlightened," she said. "Or still controlling but with a hint of basil."

"I suppose we'll see in about two hours," Abigail replied. That was what the label on the bottle had indicated.

A stroke of luck had landed the key to Abigail's plan in her possession. After Amelia's store thief was arrested, Sheriff Clark had searched the man's room at Baker's. He'd discovered pill bottles under the mattress, but later, when Abigail was changing the sheets, she'd found another bottle hidden in the pillowcase. Its label had identified the substance as chloral hydrate and detailed its use as a sedative.

Abigail had decided to keep the drug in case a boarder—or even she herself—needed it one day. As it turned out, a 500-milligram dose dissolved in lemonade was exactly what was needed on this sunny day in November. Abigail wasn't proud of pieing Ida, but she felt the self-proclaimed "upper crust" in town deserved it for the miserable way she treated people . . . and tomato plants. Heck, maybe she even did the woman a favor. Perhaps Ida *needed* a nap after all that protesting.

As Merle and Boone picked up empty glasses poking up from the sand, Belle pulled Abigail aside and nodded toward Ida. "If I'm counting correctly, this is your second secret mission this year."

Abigail brought her palm to her chest and feigned offense. "Me?" But then she whispered in Belle's ear. "You know *all* my secrets."

Belle grinned. "I sure hope you have some energy left to help me plan a not-so-secret mission."

Tapping the side of her head, Abigail replied, "I've reserved my most inventive ideas for you, honey."

Chapter 37

By December, temperatures had dipped to the midseventies, perfect for an afternoon wedding beside the Caloosahatchee. A small coconut grove along the river created a cozy cove for the upcoming ceremony, a brief affair with a small number of people. Very soon, under a canopy of feathery palm fronds, Pastor Peck would officiate as guests enjoyed the nuptials and a stunning view of the sparkling water.

"Um . . . that's a horse," Belle noted, watching Abigail enter the cottage carrying a large wooden creature.

"It just arrived at Baker's," Abigail said. She set down the toy with a thud. "Here's the card."

Belle stopped fiddling with the wedding dress laid out beside her and got up off the bed. She took the envelope and studied the small steed. The narrow, carved horse stood on two wooden rails about a yard long. "Go-Go Hoss" was stamped across one of the rails and "Edison Wood Products, Inc." was featured in smaller letters beside it. The horse was hand-painted with a brown mane and matching saddle decorated with two stars and a broad cinch. Its head was at eye level with Belle's knees.

"He's quite handsome," Belle said, and pet the horse's hard head.

"Open it," Abigail prompted, pointing at the card.

Belle did, and then held out the letter so they could both read it.

Dear Belle,

Mr. Edison and I offer our sincere congratulations regarding your upcoming wedding. I chose this toy as a hopeful wish toward your future as a mother. Your friend Alice Bishop clearly seems to think motherhood would suit you. She was quite impressed with your handling of the "tomato girls." In her letter to me, Alice wrote extensively about her little dog, but she also shared her fondness for you and her fellow members of the Circle Club. Virginia also thinks the world of your special group, and you. In my response to Alice, I encouraged her to continue valuing the company of others—both two- and four-legged—as fellowship is one of life's most precious blessings.

In closing, Belle, I do hope Go-Go has arrived in time for the celebration, and again, Mr. Edison and I extend our warmest wishes.

Kindly,
Mina

"Well, how *very* dear of the Edisons," Belle said. "And of Alice," she added, truly touched by her friend's observation. Those four words—"motherhood would suit you"—may as well have been a warm hand leading her toward a meaningful future, a life that included her not only guiding young women but—even more importantly—raising children of her own. She folded the note and slipped it back into the envelope. "What a special gift."

Abigail agreed, then added, "And you can hang Boone's drawers on Go-Go until those babies arrive." She dragged the horse to a corner. "Now let's get you dressed."

"How are things out there?" Belle asked, slipping her arms through the holes in the white linen dress Amelia had made. Buttons sewn on the back matched the "stone" on Belle's ring. Hours earlier, Merle had given her the necklace Clara was once supposed to wear at their wedding: a silver chain that held a locket. Poppy had placed sawdust-sized orchid seeds—symbols of love and fertility—inside.

As Abigail updated Belle on wedding preparations, members of the Circle Club began to stream through the door, followed by Fae and then Mazie.

"Six, seven, and eight of us women," Abigail counted, "and two girls." She shut the door and concluded, "Plus one horse. Excellent."

"How can we help?" Sadie asked, scooting aside to make room for her friends. All of them were wearing cream-colored dresses with pale-pink sashes. Abigail had declined a sash for her indiscernible waist and instead wore a wrist corsage that featured blush roses.

"Quit squirming," Fae commanded her sister. Mazie stuck her tongue out and turned her back on everyone. The girls were wearing their tomato club dresses and floral hoops atop their heads. Hazel began to fiddle with both hoops, smoothing the ribbons that hung down the girls' backs. Each one carried a small watering can filled with deep-pink bougainvillea blooms.

"I'll leave it to Mitchell to say a prayer for you and Boone," Poppy said, and gave Belle a hug. She whispered "God bless you both" in her ear.

Paulette and Sadie squatted down to assist Belle with her

shoes. She didn't need any help but let them slip on her flat white boots anyway.

"All right, time to go," Alice said when she saw Mazie stealing blooms from Fae's watering can. "Out."

"Yes. Everyone out," Abigail directed with a short whistle, pointing toward the door.

The group filed out, offering best wishes as they passed by the bride-to-be.

Once they were gone, Belle took a deep breath and sat down on the bed. Coquina wandered out from underneath and stretched.

"You can still catch the one o'clock steamer if you hurry," Abigail joked. She sat down next to Belle. "Doing all right?"

"Yes," Belle said, touching the locket on her necklace. "I'm just thinking about Clara . . . and my mother . . . and Boone's family . . ."

Abigail reached over and put her hand on Belle's. "Honey, I've known you since you were fourteen. I love that you're always thinking of others, but today . . . consider putting yourself at the top of that list."

Belle smiled. "You're one to talk." She squeezed Abigail's hand. "Thank you for everything."

"Of course," Abigail answered. "Now, what do you think those two fools of ours are up to?"

• • •

Merle was reaching up with comblike fingers, but Boone blocked the awkward attempt to tame his unruly curls.

"Nope," Boone insisted, and pushed down Merle's large hand. "My hair is like a tumbleweed. It's meant to roam free."

"Good," Merle said, "because I have no idea what I'm supposed to be doing to help."

Boone grabbed two shot glasses off the counter in Baker's.

"Now you're talkin'," Merle said, and snagged a whiskey bottle from Abigail's jelly cupboard.

As the men toasted, a group of boarders walked through the kitchen. "Looks like we're underdressed, Clyde," one man said to another. "What's the occasion, fellas?"

Merle poked his thumb toward Boone. "He's marrying an angel today."

A woman in the group squealed. "Oh, how wonderful!" She then pointed at Boone's hair and pretended to primp her own, encouraging him.

Merle threw up his hands and laughed. "I tried!"

The boarders guffawed and headed out the kitchen door and into the sunny day.

Merle yanked on each end of his ribbon tie. "I think it's real nice that your family is back together."

Boone shrugged. "We're trying." He stuck his fingertips in the short pockets of his vest. "What all did Belle tell you?"

Merle walked their glasses over to the sink. "Just that your brother was shot by a rustler. That his death was tough on everyone." He turned back toward Boone. "And that you have a nephew."

Boone grinned. "Wyatt. He looks just like my brother. I hope you can meet him one day."

"Count on it," Merle said, reaching out his hand. "Proud of you, son."

Boone shook Merle's hand, then pulled him in for a hug. "I know how lucky I am, Merle."

When the men parted, Merle gestured toward the screen door. "Let's go see your girl."

• • •

The Edisons' yard was quiet but for soft waves caressing the shoreline and the occasional cries of seagulls gliding like tiny white kites over the Caloosahatchee. In the coconut grove, Pastor Peck stood with his back to the river, clutching a Bible. To his right, the Circle Club ladies formed a line, holding hands. On the pastor's left, Boone stood facing the water to avoid getting a too-early glimpse of Belle. Decker was next to Boone, his usual grumpy frown replaced with a grin. He was staring at Virginia, seated across the makeshift aisle from Clay and Edwina. Gus and Grace Bailey rounded out the small group of guests.

"Don't they all look so wonderful?" Edwina whispered to Clay. Both had swiveled in their seats to see the bride and her helpers. "I think it's almost time," Clay said.

Abigail was standing at the start of the aisle beside Merle, Belle, and the Dawson girls. "Go ahead," she said, gently launching Fae and Mazie forward with her hands.

Merle leaned over to Abigail. "You're lovelier than ever," he murmured. She playfully wiggled her shoulders at him, and he grinned.

As the two sisters walked beside each other, they scattered the bougainvillea and stood up straight, as Paulette had instructed. When they passed by their aunt and uncle, both dropped extra flowers beside their chairs. Once the watering cans were empty, the older women welcomed the girls into their line.

Next, Abigail gave Merle and Belle a peck on the cheek and made her own way down the aisle. Her pace was uncharacteristically slow for someone who was always so busy, an exception she'd promised Merle she would make for this event. As she passed Grace Bailey, she took the woman's outstretched hand and squeezed it, the old friends clearly moved by witnessing Belle reach this milestone. She dabbed at her eyes with a hanky as she took her place beside the other women.

Merle and Belle stood next to each other. When the pastor

nodded at him, Merle offered her his arm. "Are you ready, honey?"

"Just a minute longer," she said.

Belle wanted to soak up the scene for a moment. Before her was something she never could have imagined as a child: people who loved her, people who inspired her, a good man who wanted to fold her into his future. *She* was getting married today, surrounded by everyone dearest to her, even Decker, who'd agreed to holding the ceremony in the Edisons' yard. Perhaps Boone had asked Decker to stand beside him as thanks for that allowance. Or maybe he'd felt obligated after his long absence. No matter the reason, Decker being part of the ceremony seemed meaningful, too. Everything did—the gentle bend in the palm tree trunks, the wharf stretching toward eventual sunset, a generous breeze carrying the girls' giggles to her ears.

Belle took a deep breath. She fluffed her bouquet of rain lilies and stood straighter. "Ready," she said, and looped her arm through Merle's.

Now covered with bougainvillea blooms, the "aisle" was made of bamboo poles laid end to end in the sand. Belle took her time, stepping slowly and scanning faces in the small crowd. To her left, purple Cattleya orchids bloomed in a jackfruit tree, their ruffled petals fancy and vibrant. The sky was vast and blue, capping the yard in a cloudless dome. Somewhere close, house wrens traded chirps and cheery songs. Belle marveled at the magical setting, and at the presence of everything and everyone she valued most. At that moment, her heart seemed as full as the billowed sails she could see collecting wind along the river.

"It's perfect," she said to Merle as they walked. When she looked up at him, he was smiling ear to ear, but tears were streaming down his face. Belle pulled him closer and then turned her head and locked eyes with Boone.

• • •

Boone was finally facing his bride. She looked radiant and as beautiful as ever as she walked toward him, tucked up against her very first hero. How grateful he was to Merle for saving Belle, and—in so doing, by Fate's good graces—saving him, too. He could only imagine what the kind and stalwart man was feeling as he and Belle approached and then stood before him and the pastor.

"I love you, Belley," Merle said, and kissed her cheek.

She put her arms up and hugged him, her bouquet covering one of his ears. "My life is better in a million ways because of you, Merle," she said in his free ear.

"Mine too, honey," Merle said. He let her go and went to stand beside Decker.

Belle handed her lilies to Abigail and smoothed her dress. She then turned to face Boone.

Pastor Peck said softly, "Take each other's hands."

Boone did as he was told and gazed at Belle while stroking her fingertips. Her hair was loose and wavy, reaching well past her shoulders. Behind one ear, she'd tucked a rain lily, her favorite flower. When she'd shared with him last year that the plant was known for exploding with blooms after a heavy rainstorm, he'd said, "They're beautiful and strong, just like you." Now he was about to marry this extraordinary woman, his beautiful Belle, the love of his life. He'd nearly lost her, but God or destiny, or perhaps the power of forgiveness, had intervened, and now she was nearly his wife.

"That's quite a dress, beautiful," he said quietly. It was his first time seeing her in such elegant clothing. Amelia had designed the dress with a fitted bodice to accentuate Belle's slender waistline. Its scooped neck set off the silver locket Merle had given her for her wedding day.

Belle smiled and drew his hand to her lips, lightly kissing the top of it.

The tender gesture made him want to scoop her up into his arms, but instead he simply stood facing her, his heart aglow.

•••

Pastor Peck led Belle and Boone through their vows as everyone looked on. When a tear trickled down Boone's face at one point, Sadie elbowed Amelia and whispered, "I *told* you so."

Standing adjacent to the couple, Decker awkwardly tried to hand Boone a handkerchief, but he batted it away. Belle reached over and took the hankie instead, wiping away her own tears as she and Boone made their sacred promises to each other.

When it was time for the kiss, a breeze blew strands of Belle's hair over her face, so Boone reached over and brushed them away. His hand stayed on her cheek, and he drew her to him. As they kissed, in no rush to finish, guests murmured their support. When the couple finally parted and turned to face the crowd, Alice yelled, "Hooray for the Larkins!" The entire group then clapped and cheered, a fine start to the celebration ahead.

•••

The wedding site quickly transformed into the perfect setting for a party. The men hauled over tables from Baker's, and the women went to work laying tablecloths and setting out dishes. Abigail had cooked for two days, determined to prepare all of Belle's and Boone's favorites. She'd enlisted the help of the root-cutting Finnegan boys, assigning them potato-peeling duty as punishment. She'd informed the pair they'd be on weeding duty, too, whenever the Tomato Club planted their next crop.

Before long, the savory spread was laid out—steaming bowls of venison stew, collard greens with ham hocks, and creamy mashed potatoes. Wire-mesh cloches from Belle's potting shed helped stave off pests. Small crocks of herb butter were set out beside cutting boards piled with bread, and mismatched pitchers held sweet tea and sliced lemons.

A small round table was reserved for the wedding cake, an elaborate three-tiered creation that Abigail had topped with fresh raspberries, dazzling against the chocolate icing. She'd piped small dollops of white frosting around each tier to make the cake appear as if it were stacked with pearl necklaces. Fresh flowers donated by the Baileys cascaded down the entire work of art, ending at the glass cake stand. Decker had granted Abigail's request to borrow the Edisons' elegant silver cake cutter, and it lay at the ready to slice the special dessert.

More guests had joined the post-ceremony party and were moving through the food line. Some were already seated at tables along the river.

"I cooked *all* of this," Paulette said, nodding toward the food and flashing a dazzling smile at Duke, whose plate was loaded with stew. The smithy laughed at the obvious fib and grabbed a set of silverware for them both.

Duke had just arrived, along with Hazel's beau, John, and Sadie's husband, Virgil. Abigail had prepared enough food to feed dozens more. The newlyweds had been urged to serve themselves first, so they were already sitting at their table, waiting for others to fill their plates. Abigail and Merle were waiting with them.

"Don't get any ideas," Abigail said, looking down at Merle. "We've only been out together once."

Merle was on one knee, picking up a napkin that had dropped to the ground. He chuckled and retook his seat next to hers. "And I've got a doozy of a special day planned for next time," he said. Whispering so only she could hear, he added, "Prepare to let down that bun of yours, my gal."

Belle leaned over into Boone. Several times already, she'd noticed him looking toward the driveway, presumably in search of his parents arriving for a surprise visit. Boone had told her that cows and costs had kept them at home, but she knew he was still holding out hope. "They sent us a lovely gift, honey," Belle offered.

A beautiful pine bowl, shaped like a cross, had arrived. The note from his parents read, "For your daily bread."

Boone reached over and took her hand. "I know. I just want them to meet you."

Belle smiled. "Don't worry. Mrs. Larkin will meet Mrs. Larkin before too long."

Finally, everyone was seated and enjoying the meal. People who got up for seconds made sure to stop by Abigail's table and compliment her tasty fare.

"Just make sure to save room for cake," she advised them all.

After the Circle Club members cleared dishes, Belle and Boone stood side by side next to the round table. He took a few raspberries off the cake's top tier and popped them into his mouth.

"Don't make me cut your fingers off," Belle teased as she picked up the silver knife and waved it at him. She then began to cut generous slices of the vanilla cake. A line began to form at the table, and Fae and Mazie were right up front.

"We can help, Miss Belle," Fae said. "I can carry two pieces and so can Mazie."

Belle handed the girls cake. "Very helpful. Thank you, ladies." Boone set out more plates for Belle to fill.

Next in line were Virginia and Decker, standing arm in arm. "Here we go," Boone said under his breath.

"I'll take this one," Decker said, choosing a large wedge of cake. He held it up so Virginia could see the decorative strings of frosting. "Pearls for Miss Virginia Pearl."

Virginia smiled and took the plate. "You spoil me, Norville."

Boone pushed a slice toward the mooning caretaker. "Let's keep the line moving."

Belle put her hand on Boone's arm and addressed Decker herself. "There's no rush, Norville." She looked at Virginia. "We can't thank you enough for coming all this way."

Virginia said, "Of course. Getting a glimpse of true love is rare, you know."

Decker beamed and held a forkful of Virginia's cake up to her mouth. "'The sight of lovers feedeth those in love,'" he crooned.

Virginia held up her hand, blocking the fork. "Let's sit down, Norville."

"Oh, God bless you, Virginia," Boone said. When Belle kicked his boot under the table, he added, "And thanks for everything, Decker."

As guests continued to accept cake and offer their congratulations, a trio of men began to play music; Virgil, Duke, and John had taken up a banjo, fiddle, and guitar to get the crowd moving. Before long, everyone was either dancing or tapping along to the two-four time of a spirited polka. Belle and Boone did their best to keep up, unfamiliar with the footing. They laughed, stepped on each other's toes, and nearly tripped over one another. Poppy and Pastor Peck stole the show, their pace and precision admirable.

When the lively tempo slowed to a steady waltz, even more people paired up to join the fun. Alice took to the sandy dance floor with Coconut and dipped the dog dramatically toward the ground several times. One of the most captivating sights of the evening was Virginia, affixed to Decker. Her stocky body was moving with such grace and poise that one half expected to see her begin dancing *en pointe*. Habitually toadish, Decker somehow appeared downright princely when he was around Virginia and whenever a band began to play. Now, with both at his disposal, the man seemed to sparkle.

When the sun began to set over the Caloosahatchee, Abigail suggested they move the party to Front Street, "under the lights." In a surprise move, Merle directed guests to several horse-drawn buckboards waiting to transport them to town. The lead wagon was decorated on all four sides with a garland of fragrant honeysuckle woven through grapevine. A bouquet of sunflowers lay on the bench seat for Belle, a shot of whiskey for Boone.

"Up you go," Merle said, and helped Belle onto the wagon. Boone hopped up on the other side and downed the hooch.

Abigail came to stand beside Merle. "Let's all go have a little more fun, Postmaster," she said, and wrapped her arm around his waist. Merle had submitted the paperwork required to strip Ida of her position with the post office and regain his.

"The *real* fun begins for you soon," Merle said, winking at Boone.

Boone smiled and took the reins. "Giddyap," he said, then lightly tapped the horse's backside. Belle buried her nose in the sunflowers to hide her blushing cheeks.

Chapter 38

The next day, Belle and Boone took off for Sarasota, having decided to return to the luxurious DeSoto and pick up where they left off behind the pillar. Scarlet Smeltzer would be elsewhere this time, holed up in her fancy home or looking down her nose at someone else around town. But she was the last thing on their minds as they walked through the tall doors of the lobby.

Windows in their sizable hotel room faced the bay and opened outward. A fresh breeze and the soothing *clip-clop* of horse-drawn buggies floated in. Candles on a table and both dressers flickered, their soft light soon to replace that of the setting sun. Belle and Boone had eaten a light meal in the hotel's dining room and were now standing beside the wide, soft bed.

"We'll take it slow, love," Boone said, and kissed his new bride. The two spoke in hushed voices for a few moments more. Boone then reached down for the hem of her dress and gently began to inch it up. "Is this all right?" he asked.

She nodded and helped him lift it up and over her head, revealing an ivory slip that Paulette had lent her. The bust was too big, which Belle knew. Still, she thought the intimate night called for something special. Boone laid both his palms on the soft fabric covering her breasts.

"I don't quite fill this out," she said, placing her hands over his.

Boone leaned over and kissed her neck. "You're perfect." He scooped her up and carried her to the bed.

Belle began to wonder why she'd lit so many candles, knowing that she'd soon lay undressed. "Tell me what to do," she said quietly.

Boone ran his fingers through her hair as he lay beside her. "When you're ready, let me see what's under that silk." The sheets were pulled back, allowing them to see each other from head to ankle. "But I'm happy to look at you just like this for a while."

After several minutes, she decided it was time to reveal more of him. One by one, she undid buttons on his shirt and then ran her hands inside it, caressing his chest. His skin was warm and soft, so she kissed it all the way down to his belt buckle.

When she looked up at him, he said, "My turn." He slipped off his shirt, unbuckled his belt, and shimmied out of his pants.

Belle studied Boone's body, trim and strong. She now saw, in the flesh, what she'd touched through his clothing many times before. As she watched his excitement grow, her nervousness gave way to arousal. She held her arms up over her head, and Boone responded, slowly removing the silk slip. When he reached for her necklace to take it off, too, she pressed her fingers over the locket.

"Leave it on," she said softly, imagining the orchid seeds inside.

Voices of people strolling along the bay wafted through the windows, yet Belle and Boone were too entwined to hear anything but each other's heavy breathing. They kissed with more passion than they ever had before, shifting positions on the bed to better please each other. As Boone explored Belle's body, he asked softly, "Glad you didn't cut off my fingers?"

She moaned and leaned into him.

• • •

Afterward, she lay in Boone's arms and listened to him lightly snore. She was relaxed but not ready to sleep. Instead, she thought about a drawing Boone had included in the letter he'd mailed her from Kissimmee. At the time, she'd been angry with him and was interested only in the return address. But after she'd received his telegram explaining the Tilly letters, she'd finally read the note.

As she stared at the ceiling, she reflected on that difficult time. While she was crumbling—certain he'd traveled home to his secret family—Boone had been drafting plans for *their* family home. On the back of the letter, he'd drawn a simple structure surrounded by a yard. He even sketched her potting shed and a square flower garden beside it. The house featured five rooms, and in capital letters he'd labeled one of them *BABIES*.

Tears trickled down her cheeks now, her soul awash with relief and thankfulness. Never, as a child, had she imagined that her dark world would one day be as bright as tonight's moon over the bay. She couldn't have known that throughout her trying journey, Joy was waiting patiently to meet her one day. Now, finally, she was learning to trust that everything was unfolding as it should, that life would never reveal its plans ahead of time, and that, perhaps, was for the best.

Boone stirred and turned his head toward her. "You all right?" he mumbled.

She stroked his cheek and said softly, "Yes, Boone. Everything is so right."

Chapter 39

In October 1890, the *Press* reported a variety of local news items in the Announcements section. One in particular would be clipped and displayed with overwhelming joy inside Duggan's general store and Baker's Boarding.

> Miss Flossie Hill entertained a party
> of ladies and gentlemen at her home
> last Friday night for a rousing game
> of whist. Refreshments included lem-
> onade, a variety of cakes, and coconut
> cookies.

> For sale.
> Five head of healthy Farm and
> Family horses—also a pair of good
> mules. See H. E. Heitman.

> "Lucky Jones" landed a seven-foot

silver king on Friday the thirteenth,
the dire combination of day and date
not potent enough to offset Jones's
luck. Harry L. Newman also brought a
big fighter to gaff.

Mr. and Mrs. Boone Larkin welcomed
their first child, Eva Daniela. Both
parents are employed by Prof. Thos.
A. Edison. Mr. Larkin has built their
new home on a spacious parcel behind
Duggan's general store.

Chapter 40

Belle knew that when a daydream comes true, the real version often lacks the luster of its flawless performance in the mind. But today, that was not the case. As she sat gazing down at her swaddled sleeping bundle, the weight and warmth seemed familiar. She'd often pictured herself cuddling a baby, cooing down toward a blanket, and now, here she was, doing just that. Still, she had *never* dared dream about the love she'd feel one day for a child. The imagination was simply not designed to conjure something so intense and profound.

"I love you, Eva," she whispered to the six-month-old, who'd just fallen asleep, despite the conversations underway around her.

"You don't have to be too quiet," Sadie advised the group. "Babies need to learn to sleep no matter how much noise is going on." She eyed Abigail chopping walnuts in the kitchen.

"I'm almost done," Abigail said, her knife blade banging against a cutting board.

Circle Club meetings were now permanently held at the Larkin home, which had been finished just a week before Eva's birth. Boone had run himself ragged trying to wrap up work on their five-room house, and thanks to his efforts—and help from Merle, Gus Bailey, and Mr. Ritter—Eva came into the world with a completed roof over her tiny head. Every birth was a worrisome ordeal, and Eva's was no different. The fact that Belle's mother had died delivering Belle had added to the unease. Thankfully, baby and mama had not only survived, but both were now healthy, content, and surrounded by people who loved them dearly.

"I just can't believe I'm getting married," Hazel gushed, looking down at the substantial diamond ring John Parker had slipped on her finger last week. A rose cut, the stone was flat at the bottom with a faceted prism dome.

"And now you'll be married to Polk's, too," Amelia quipped, sitting in a rocker, knitting a baby blanket. Her skills were so good and her eyes so bad that she'd taught herself to knit without looking down. "Ida can't keep you from me now."

"John says he doesn't mind if I keep working," Hazel said, spinning in a circle to show each person her ring. "And he'd better not!"

When Hazel's hand passed by Alice, the girl grabbed it. She then dropped to one knee and pretended she was John. "Oh, my darling, when your mother moves in with us . . ."

Hazel slapped at Alice's hand and yanked hers away. "Never ever!"

Paulette laughed and stroked Coquina as the cat passed by her chair. "Your ring is gorgeous, Hazel."

"And so is yours, Paulette," Hazel answered warmly.

Several days ago, Duke had given her a beautifully crafted silver-spoon ring as a token of his adoration. The unique piece of jewelry featured a delicate flower pattern and three loops that encircled and accentuated Paulette's long, slim fingers. Her reenactment of the "saucer eyes" Duke had made when she playfully slipped the ring on her wedding finger had fully entertained the other women.

Abigail entered the sitting room, wiping her hands on her apron. "I've got cookies in the oven, ladies." She'd decided to attend meetings now, having discovered that her boarders did just fine for an hour or two with coffee on the stove and a plate of cornbread or sweets left out in her absence. Plus, the new boarder in the Edison cottage—a retired schoolteacher—was happy to help out in a pinch. Abigail leaned over Belle to lightly stroke the baby's soft forehead. "How is she doing?"

Belle stifled a yawn. "She's tired."

"I meant the baby," Abigail joked. She kissed Belle on the head.

"Let's just sit around and yap today," Sadie suggested, putting her feet up on a tufted round ottoman. "I just don't feel like being productive, friends."

"Fellowship *is* productive," Poppy offered, while folding shirts and pants she'd plucked off the clothesline. Boone had strung several lines between two trellises in the backyard so Belle could look at flowering vines as she hung or took down laundry. This afternoon, fragrant wild passionflowers were blooming on both sets of lattice. Coconut was napping elsewhere, tucked up next to the pretty little potting shed now set up in the Larkin's front yard.

Belle laid her head back on the chair and closed her eyes. She and Boone were both exhausted and deliriously happy. They thought Eva was perfect. Of course, Merle and Abigail agreed. Boone's parents were saving up to visit sometime in the weeks ahead and hoped to bring Wyatt. Belle had prepared a room for them and for any other overnight guests. Virginia would always be welcome, though Belle knew that Abigail might prefer she stay at Baker's. Clearly, Norville would. How wonderful to have a friend so lovely that everyone wanted her nearby.

Plenty remained to be done to decorate the house, but Belle had already hung curtains and rearranged furniture until every item found its proper place. Clay had built a sturdy dresser for Eva's room as well as a cozy crib, complete with a whirligig like the one outside his shop. Eva was fascinated by the little boats, especially whenever Belle served as the wind, spinning the small fleet attached to the crib's side rail. Edwina was still dropping by regularly with food, a blessing and truly a treat. Her pork pot pies were their favorite.

Both Belle and Boone continued to work at the Edison property. Belle had enjoyed a brief break but now took the baby with her unless the weather didn't cooperate; in that case, Abigail, Merle, or Grace Bailey were happy to watch Eva. But on pretty days, Belle tucked her daughter inside a blanketed woven basket, where she napped or spent time learning what her chubby limbs could do. Belle would give her something to grasp, like a lime or a small ball of garden twine, simple objects that seemed to fascinate Eva.

Inside the house, she often sat the child on Go-Go Hoss and held on to her. Eva would slap the sides of the horse's neck and murmur cute baby noises. Boone loved to walk through every room, holding their daughter, pointing out particulars during the tour. "Mama's plants . . . Papa's coffee cup . . . Eva's dress." He rarely napped without her on his chest, Eva's arms and legs stretched out like the limbs of a turtle.

When Belle heard someone enter the house, she opened her eyes.

"Hello, ladies," Boone said, standing in the hallway.

The women greeted him as Abigail appeared from the kitchen, carrying a plate full of warm walnut cookies.

"Never fails," she said, and shook her head at Boone.

"What . . . ?" he said, winking at the other club members. "I just happened to arrive now."

"I swear he can smell when they're done," Abigail said, offering cookies to Boone.

He grabbed one with each hand. "Thank you and thank you." He made quick work of both and approached Belle.

As the ladies passed around the plate of treats, Belle tipped her head back to accept a peck on the lips.

"We're just yapping today," Belle told him. "No real club business."

Boone sat down on an embroidered footstool next to Belle's chair. "Seems like you're all set for the bake sale, so why not take it easy?"

The women were hoping to bake their way into earning enough money to buy modern canning equipment for the Tomato Club. A half-dozen girls had joined up since the tomato festival, and at Belle's request, Alice was now teaching new members about the club's goals.

"I'll take her so you can rest, sweetheart," Boone said, standing. He scooped up the baby and held her above Belle for a moment.

"Thanks," she said, and gently grasped Eva's little pink toes as she dangled overhead. "Sleep well, my angel."

Boone headed for the baby's room, clutching Eva against his chest. Relaxed and groggy, Belle closed her eyes and listened to the women chat and chuckle. The house smelled like butter, and a spring breeze floated through an open window behind her. As she drifted off to sleep, Belle thanked God for answering her repeated prayer, and instead of asking for anything more, she simply surrendered.

God, I trust your plan.

Chapter 41

Like two queens of twilight, Fae and Mazie promenaded down adjacent dirt rows, lush green plants between them. The pair liked to wander the patch before dusk, surveying the harvest and upholding their positions as "original" Tomato Club members. For the past two months, they'd worked hard for their kingdom of perfect Paragons, every vine now heavy with blush tomatoes. Soon the healthy crop would be red and ripe for picking. The new girls in the club treated Fae and Mazie as if they were in charge, which was exciting, but they, too, were still learning plenty about the art of growing and canning prize-worthy tomatoes.

"Hold on a minute," Mazie directed.

She stopped and leaned over one of the plants, examining the white fuzz poking out from its thick stem and deep-green leaves.

"Yep. Our plants are as hairy as your legs, Fae," she said, and then dashed off, expecting retaliation.

But Fae just kept walking and spoke loudly to her fleeing sister. "Miss Belle says they're called trichomes. Tiny hairs that help protect the plant from disease and pests," she explained, ignoring her sister's attempt at humor. "*You're* a pest!" she yelled.

As Fae watched, Mazie began to pretend she was a kite, sailing through the field with her arms outstretched. She stopped now and then to right a leaning bamboo stake and then continued her imaginary flight. At that moment, Fondness tucked itself up against Fae's heart. As much as her younger sister sometimes annoyed her, Mazie was also a comfort. Her light-brown eyes were kind and aware, ready to console at the first sign of distress. And both girls were still experiencing bouts of sadness; some days together, some when only one of them would seek a quiet place where tears and memories could flow freely. Uncle Clay and Aunt Edwina continued to love them through everything, and the sisters had made a secret pact to help more and bicker less. Their aunt's hair had seemed to turn a more silver shade of gray since they'd arrived, and they supposed they were to blame.

"Can you believe our field is full of tomatoes, Sissy?" Mazie said. She'd glided back to where Fae was standing.

"Do you suppose they'll mind living in tiny cans after all of this?" Fae asked, her arms held wide open.

Mazie giggled and began spinning around like a dirt devil, her dusty boots flinging soil in all directions.

Fae watched her whirling sister and drew in a deep breath, content in the moment. Soon they'd be sitting around the supper table, eating one of Aunt Edwina's delicious meals. Tomorrow they'd visit little Eva and take turns holding her while Miss Belle worked in her beloved gardens. And then would come their weekly canning class with the Circle Club. Slowly but surely, Fae was learning that it was a lot easier to spot sunshine if you didn't let the dark clouds boss you around.

"Ready?" Mazie asked. She'd stopped spinning.

"Ready," Fae answered, and the girls began to walk across the patch toward Polk's. Fae grinned as she admired the rows and rows of perfect soil, rendered weedless by the naughty, root-slashing Finnegan boys.

"Let's say an extra prayer tonight for all our blessings," Fae suggested, moving closer to her sister.

Mazie took Fae's hand and squeezed it. "Yes! And the night after that, and the night after that . . ."

The girls began to repeat the phrase in unison, over and over, laughing and skipping as they neared the road home.

Dear Reader

Perhaps somewhere, there is a particular place that has charmed and claimed you. For me, that place is Thomas Edison's winter estate in southwest Florida.

As I explained at the end of my previous novel, *After the Rain*, I became captivated by the Edison property more than thirty years ago, during my career as a broadcast journalist. While working as a television reporter and anchor in Fort Myers, I shadowed a horticulturist who cared for the Edisons' expansive gardens, filled with botanical specimens from all over the world. During the tour, we wandered past blooming trees, butter-yellow homes, and the inventor's intriguing laboratory. Extraordinary! Decades later, I was inspired to create characters and a story that illuminated what may have transpired there in 1888.

After the release of my debut novel, I couldn't seem to shake my main character, Belle Carson, and her pals. I missed them! While fiction writers often yearn to hang out again in the worlds they've built, a sequel is not always advised. Still, after much consideration, I decided to go forth, determined not to drop a disappointment bomb on readers who'd already met my cast of characters. My plan began to crystallize when I happened upon a little-known turn-of-the-century movement featured in a magazine.

Because my health insurance provider was originally formed to serve agricultural communities, the quarterly publication sent to subscribers like me is filled with stories about farmers, small towns, and all the warm and fuzzy topics I love. When I came across an article explaining the girls' tomato club movement in the rural South, I dog-eared it, intrigued. *How many other people don't know about this interesting chapter in American history?* I soon learned that these early youth clubs—boys farming corn and girls growing tomatoes—were the precursors to our more well-known 4-H clubs of today. The original motto remains in use by 4-H: "To make the best better."

I began to map out a way to incorporate a girls' tomato club into Belle's 1889 Fort Myers. (The club movement actually gained traction around 1910, but I was certain you'd indulge me.) As I dived into researching Virginia P. Moore, Tennessee's first pioneer in the tomato club movement, I nearly fell off my chair. Included in the University of Tennessee's Virginia Moore digital collection was a photo of Thomas Edison standing with Virginia Moore beside beehives! Then I found another point of connection: Virginia posing with Mina Edison in front of the Edisons' winter estate! No dates were listed, but it didn't matter. My idea to bring Virginia Moore to Fort Myers to talk tomatoes was now not at all far-fetched.

When I corresponded with a UT archivist, she speculated that Virginia probably met Mina during summer visits to the Chautauqua Institution in New York. She explained, too, that Miss Moore moved to Florida in 1923 and perhaps continued her friendship with the Edison family. Even without clear answers about when or why Virginia was associated with the Edisons, discovering their connection felt magical to me. UT's extensive digital collection also offered me an invaluable glimpse into the tomato club girls' charming booklets—their challenges, triumphs, and darling handwriting.

As in my first novel, I chose to keep the Edisons' involvement in the story limited, my focus instead on the main cast and their personal growth. Along with Thomas and Mina, characters in the book who retained the names of their real-life inspirations are (in order of appearance): Virginia P. Moore, C. J. Huelsenkamp, Mrs. S. Watson, Marshal David Bass, Ethelee Scott (girl on left in back cover photo), Professor James Ricalton, and H. E. Heitman. Abigail's inventor background was inspired by Margaret Knight, a prolific American creator known as the "woman Edison" of her time. In 1871, she—unlike Abigail—won her patent interference lawsuit against the machinist who tried to steal her design for a flat-bottomed paper bag.

While I loved writing about Abigail's success with the dynamo, the townspeople of Fort Myers didn't enjoy electricity until 1898. And alas, Edison played no role in the process. In October 1897, the frustrated town council contracted with the Seminole Canning Company to furnish Fort Myers with ten incandescent lights. Then on New Year's Day, the newspaper reported that "a soft light suddenly appeared in all the stores and houses connected with the electric light plant, and for the first time, electricity was used as lighting power in Lee County." But it's more fun to think that Abigail won the day, isn't it?

My final clarification involves "Go-Go Hoss," the wedding gift from the Edisons. The original toy horse, named Go-Go Hos, was part of the Edison Little Folks Furniture line manufactured from 1937 to 1969 by Edison Wood Products. I didn't think you'd mind if I saddled up Go-Go a few decades early.

Now that I've completed two novels set in Fort Myers, the Edison property is even more meaningful to me. Should you ever be in southwest Florida, I highly recommend a trip to the

Edison and Ford Winter Estates. If you don't have the opportunity to explore the setting in person, a virtual visit is possible, day or night. I've included the website below.

As always, dear reader, thank you for giving me a reason to share my writing and my passion for historical research. I hope my decision to write a sequel was a good one, and that *The Growing Season* in some way has brought you as much pleasure as a pantry full of canned homegrown tomatoes.

With endless gratitude,

Jane

For more information, visit edisonfordwinterestates.org.

Acknowledgments

If all goes as planned, readers will develop a meaningful connection with the fictional folks they invite into their favorite chair or airplane seat or beach lounger—wherever they choose to crack open a book. As a writer, to have the chance to launch characters from the page into a reader's mind and heart is the ultimate honor. And quite a challenge.

To the astute and gracious readers who supported me as I wrote this novel:

Candy—you printed my manuscript and created a small book that you hole-punched and bound using an ice pick and thread. Of course you did, creative one! Then, you lovingly guided me on how to best protect and polish Belle, Boone, and the whole gang. All the while, you were traveling and managing life in the sandwich generation. Thank you for giving so much to so many, including me.

Susan—you had me at "snacks and wine on the porch," and then you one-upped that with perceptive thoughts about how mothering manifests itself in all shapes and sizes. And because you expressed your affection for Fae and Mazie, mine grew, too. Thank you and cheers, pal.

John—you kindly made time for my book while you and Laurie were busy planning a new chapter in your family's life,

Iain's wedding. Thank you for suggesting where to dig deeper, and props for seeing a small typo with big implications: *thong*. I meant to write *throng* . . . a much more appropriate word for 1889. Ha.

Christine—after a long year of teaching high school English, you kindly read yet one more "paper," my manuscript. We've been sharing thoughts since grade school, so your wise insights and keen eye didn't surprise me at all. Thank you for your red pen and for decades of meaningful conversations and support.

Billy—thanks for the valuable tip on using three-by-five index cards to create an outline. Being able to move the cards around like puzzle pieces really helped! Keep writing, cowpoke.

To the people who supported me as I researched and wrote:

Laura Romans and Louisa Trott with the University of Tennessee—you both encouraged me to explore UT's digital collection honoring Virginia P. Moore. Wonderful! The site is thoughtfully curated with historic photos and documents that helped me develop Virginia's personality and fueled my passion for the tomato club movement. I pored over charming tomato club booklets created by girls from that era, their words and drawings inspiring me as I brought Fae and Mazie to life. Thank you both.

Girl Friday Productions—hooray for our second journey together! Thank you to Christina Henry de Tessan for getting the ball rolling and for assigning me a rock-star editor; Kristin Duran for having octopus arms to calmly and skillfully manage me and seven other tasks at the same time; Shari MacDonald Strong, my rock and my star, for such a meaningful and enjoyable editing process. I'm beyond grateful that GFP put my story in your capable hands and caring heart; Katherine Richards and Abi Pollokoff for so effectively overseeing the copyediting extravaganza; Wanda Zimba for your diligent sleuthing and invaluable suggestions and corrections; Carrie Wicks for expertly proofing and perfecting my tale; and Paul Barrett for once again designing an alluring cover that transports the eye to a bygone era.

Jim—it's ugly when I can't find the roadmap, isn't it? Thank you for knowing that I eventually do, and for cheering me on as I roll along, hit speed bumps, and eventually reach my destination. Two smooches this time.

Hoda—if Love came to life, she'd look just like you. Thank you for showering me with so much of it for so many years.

My parents in heaven and my sisters by my side—everything beautiful in this book springs from you. The four of you were blessed with green thumbs, but mine is merely attached to Belle. Gardening prowess is just one of the many things I admire and love about each of you.

And finally, to the internet—how would I know if pencils were available in 1889 or how Mrs. S. Watson made her tomato toast (and a million other historical details) without you?—www.thankyou.com.

About the Author

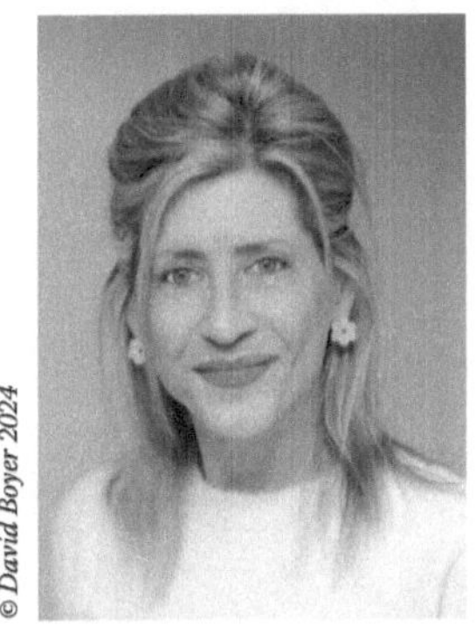

Jane Lorenzini has written professionally for nearly forty years, a third of which she spent as a television news anchor and reporter. She then became a freelance writer and a four-time *New York Times* bestselling author, cowriting five nonfiction books with dear friend and *Today* cohost Hoda Kotb. In 2018 Jane released *After the Rain*, her debut novel. *The Growing Season*, released in 2024, explores another year in the lives of her characters. Jane lives in Tennessee and writes everywhere.

www.ingramcontent.com/pod-product-compliance
Lightning Source LLC
Chambersburg PA
CBHW031443200726
48289CB00007BB/2178